Mike Farrell is a compulsive gambler...
But now even he finds the stakes too high!

A fortune in diamonds has been missing for seven years, and only the man who stole them knows where they are hidden.

Gambler Mike Farrell finds himself forced to pose as the thief as part of a desperate plot to find the gems. If he fails, he dies.

When Mike tries to unravel the tangled threads of another man's life, he finds his own life jeopardized—by a woman he can't fool, a cop he can't hate . . . and a corpse he can't hide.

SIGNET Thrillers
by *Carter Brown*

TO OUR READERS

the *carter brown*
mystery series

the
scarlet
flush

A SIGNET BOOK

published by
THE NEW AMERICAN LIBRARY
OF WORLD LITERATURE, INC.

in association with
HORWITZ PUBLICATIONS INC.

Published by arrangement with Alan G. Yates

FIRST PRINTING, OCTOBER, 1963

SIGNET TRADEMARK REG. U.S. PAT. OFF. AND FOREIGN COUNTRIES
REGISTERED TRADEMARK—MARCA REGISTRADA
HECHO EN CHICAGO, U.S.A.

SIGNET BOOKS are published by
The New American Library of World Literature, Inc.
501 Madison Avenue, New York 22, New York

PRINTED IN THE UNITED STATES OF AMERICA

the
scarlet
flush

chapter one

It was one of those dull expensive restaurants where they always overcharge for the food, and the service is lousy, anyway. For the last six weeks I had averaged four nights a week inside the place and never gotten to eat there yet. This night was no exception to the rule; I followed the usual routine of one drink at the bar before I slipped through the unmarked door tucked in back of an alcove. Then came the long hike along a winding corridor to the steel door at the end, and the creep in a dinner suit who propped up the wall like he had nothing but time and no place to spend it.

"Hi, Mr. Farrel!" He grinned, showing a couple of wide gaps between yellowed tombstones. "Feel lucky tonight, hey?"

"I feel lucky every night, hey!" I said bleakly.

He shrugged, then pressed the concealed switch so the steel door slid open. I took two steps forward—the door slid shut behind me sealing off the unreality of the outside—and I was back home again in *my* world, where the shapes of destiny were stacked in the cards, rolled with the dice, and spun with the wheel. This night I was giving destiny a limited choice; either I walked out of the room a winner who'd annexed the house, or a big loser who'd drawn the scarlet flush.

The redhead who sat in a cage all night, more protected than some secret nuclear weapon, looked at me with tired eyes and tried to smile. It was a lousy try and she gave up about halfway.

"Hello, Mr. Farrel." Her voice was cautious. "Going to try your luck again tonight?"

"Luck? What's that?" I grated.

"I don't like to say this, Mr. Farrel, but—"

"My markers aren't good anymore," I finished for her, and watched the slight look of relief show on her face. "Tonight, you don't have to worry, baby!" I opened my wallet, took out a fat wad of notes, and pushed them under the wire that separated us. "That's a grand and it buys me just twenty of those little red chips, right?"

She counted the money with professional speed, then pushed a small stack of red chips back under the wire. "Can I wish you luck, Mr. Farrel?"

"Why not?" I said. "I don't have anything else going for me right now."

I walked toward the nearest roulette wheel, clutching the small stack of chips in my hand, and my palm started to sweat gently. It didn't feel like much at all for what it represented—the last of my bank balance and the proceeds from the sale of my car after the finance company had gotten their percentage back first. My wallet felt limp with the one five-spot, which was all that stood between me and starvation once those twenty little red chips vanished. But they wouldn't, of course. After the lousy luck I'd had in the last six weeks, this had to be my night to howl.

There was a crazy-faced blonde beside me at the table wearing a low-cut dress. I figured her impossible uplift had to be a living testimony to the hidden bones and wiring inside her bodice. She gave a shrill squeal of delight as the ivory ball dropped into the zero slot. I watched the croupier quickly rake in all the other bets and looked blankly at the dame.

"Crazy!" she said. "I was riding the zero, you know that! How much does that get me, handsome?"

"Thirty-five to one," I told her. "How much did you have riding on it?"

"A couple of hundred," she said casually.

"You just made yourself seven grand, honey!" I gritted my teeth. "Wear it in good health!"

I stared at the stack of chips being pushed her way by the croupier. It was like hypnosis. Seven G's in one payoff! I'd come to this joint because it was the only roulette operation I knew of where there was no limit on bets. For the past six weeks I'd been making even-money bets, six-number bets, corner bets, column bets, but I'd stayed away from single-number bets except for once or twice. And I'd been losing my shirt. And here was this crazy-faced blonde hitting the zero at thirty-five to one! My scalp tingled and I broke into a sweat as that stack of chips came to rest in front of her.

I forced myself to look in the other direction, to my left, and found myself looking straight into a pair of sordid brown eyes. Their owner smiled with his lips, while his eyes kept right on saying something dirty, and he did mean me.

"This is a surprise, Mike," he said softly.

"Hello, Walter." I bared my teeth at him. "I paid cash for these." I opened my fingers a little so he could see the red chips. "But I guess you know that already? You're the kind of owner who never leaves anything to chance, right?"

"I'd say we left a lot to chance, in taking your markers for a total of ten grand. But we took 'em. You've got your thousand in cash, so okay. We'll hold your markers."

"Maybe it'll be different after tonight," I grunted.

"I hope so." His voice was still soft and pleasant, and his eyes kept right on talking dirty at me.

I looked him up and down slowly. He was tall, around my height, but he carried maybe thirty pounds more weight than I did and most of it around his waistline. His black hair was thinning noticeably, and his sallow skin didn't do anything to help his fleshy face, either. Walter Arndt was a creep, but that didn't make him an automatic pushover, I remembered.

"I feel exactly the same way about you, baby," I

told him. "Now, if you don't mind, I'd like to play a little roulette?"

"The customer is always right." He smiled thinly for a moment, then turned away.

I turned back to the crazy-faced blonde and her stack of chips.

"How long were you playing the zero before you hit the jackpot, honey?" I asked.

"All night it felt like," she said. "But it was twenty times, increasing my bet by ten each time. It cost me. That two hundred was the end—my last two hundred in the whole world, you know that?"

"Why don't you cash in while you're ahead?" I suggested.

"Momma's going to spread one little grand over five more tries," she said in a determined voice. "Then I quit, whatever!"

She lost her grand on the next five spins of the wheel, grabbed the still-substantial pile of chips left in both hands, and turned away from the table.

"It's all yours, handsome," she said happily. "I give you all my luck as a farewell gift. You, too, should wear it in good health!"

After she'd gone I just stood and watched the next ten spins of the wheel, without betting a dime. The zero didn't come up again, and I felt the fever bubbling in my veins like Old Faithful at Yellowstone. When you've got gambling in your bloodstream instead of red corpuscles the way I have, it only leaves you a couple of lousy little deuces in the destiny stakes. One deuce is the omen, and the other is the guts, and both operate on the superstitious illogical premise that sometime, somewhere, somehow, they'll come together for you in a combination strong enough to buck the odds, not to mention the house percentage going against you on every spin. I'd read up on roulette systems and tried a few without much conviction, only confirming what I knew already: systems are for suckers; there's no system that can beat this game. It's luck and luck alone.

The crazy-faced blonde who'd cleaned up on the zero with her last two hundred bucks was my good luck omen, okay! My scalp still prickled and my spine tingled and I felt lit up like neon. The zeroes were hot tonight—I knew it. Her payoff was on the single zero; I'd get mine on the double.

The wheel was a standard American wheel with thirty-eight slots—thirty-six numbers plus zero and double zero. Whenever zero or double zero came up, the house would collect all bets on the layout except those on zero or double zero. The law of probabilities said that zero or double zero had to come up twice in every thirty-eight spins of the wheel—in the long run. The blonde had bet twenty times on the zero before it came up, she'd said, then five more times after that before she'd quit. I had just watched the next ten spins of the wheel and the zero or double zero hadn't come up again. That made a total of thirty-five spins for the zeroes with only one payoff. Logic could have told me that my figuring had nothing to do with my possibilities of winning—probabilities are figured on the very long run. But all my logic had gone home to bed, and I was standing there bright-eyed and bushy-tailed, knowing for a fact that I could play for the short run. It was double zero, and it would come up during the next three spins.

I put two hundred bucks on the double zero for the next spin and it came up 13, only two pockets away; three hundred the next and it came up 27, right next door to double zero. What the hell? I figured it was even better this way because the last five hundred I had would be riding the certainty the next time, and I pushed the ten red chips onto the double zero with complete confidence. It came up 36. I stood there, trying to push that small ivory ball with my eyes the three slots it needed. It stayed put.

"Are you betting this time, Mr. Farrel?" the croupier asked politely.

"No, I don't think so," I mumbled at him, lit a cigarette, then walked away from the table with the

momentary intention of finding that crazy-faced
blonde and strangling her to death. I wound up at the
bar instead, and ordered a double bourbon on the
rocks which cost me two bucks. Two-fifths of my total
wealth for just one drink was a little rough, I figured,
but the bartender didn't look the sympathetic type so
it was useless to argue.

I sat there staring at my reflection in the mirror back
of the bar, indulging in that orgy of self-pity, hate, and
revulsion, which is the hallmark of the compulsive
gambler. Or that's what Julie had said, anyway. I
stared numbly at the dark satanic face that scowled
back at me from the bar mirror, and wondered if it
was only six months since I'd last seen a girl called
Julie Holland.

Was it only a few months back that I'd gotten out of
a caper with some syndicate hoods on the West Coast
that had damned nearly cost me my life, and figured I
had everything made? I was about to marry a beautiful girl called Julie who loved me, and invest the
twenty grand I had banked in some legitimate business
because I was finished with gambling for all time. So
what happened?

Julie Holland's clear blue eyes had a determined
look, I remembered, even if her softly vulnerable lower
lip had quivered a couple of times. *"With you, it's like
a disease, Mike,"* she had said in a carefully unemo-
tional voice. *"You're a compulsive gambler and you
can't stay away from it any more than an alcoholic
can stay away from the booze! It's eating away at you
the whole time, at your mind, your heart, and your
soul, even. If you don't try and beat it, it's going to
destroy you completely, and I'm not going to stay
around and watch it happen, Mike! You make a choice
right now. Either you want to go on gambling, or you
want me. You can't have both!"*

I had told her I'd think it over, and when I got back
from a poker game around four the next morning I
still hadn't made up my mind about it either way, but
by then it didn't matter anymore because Julie was

gone. So I continued right on being what I'd always been—a professional gambler—only something had happened to me when I hit this stinking town six weeks back. For no good reason I'd quit poker—the one game I knew where luck could be helped by skill —and started playing the roulette wheel like some dumb broad celebrating a divorce settlement in Reno, or something. Maybe Julie had been right with that compulsive gambler two-bit analysis. Did I really want to blow it all the time? Did I want the fizzle, the flop, the scarlet flush? Did I only gamble to lose because in some dark recess of my mind there was a load of hate and contempt for myself that was gratified by the self-inflicted humiliation of it all?

"Same again, sir?" The bartender's voice jolted me back to reality.

"And on the house this time, Joe," a soft, familiar voice said right beside me.

Walter Arndt grinned as I turned my head and looked at him. "Your luck was real bad tonight, Mike," he said like he was enjoying every word. "After you left the table, the double zero came up twice in the next five spins!"

"Since you're buying me a drink, I'll let you cry for me, too," I grated.

The bartender placed another double bourbon in front of me, and what looked like the same in front of Arndt, then moved down to the other end of the bar.

"I talked to Gilda," Arndt said conversationally.

"The redhead in the cage?" I queried. "The one with the tired eyes?"

"She's just a cashier to me, friend." His eyes glittered for a moment. "Gilda said you had a grand in cash all ready when you came in tonight."

"So?"

"So you shot that wad, and you're still into us for ten grand. What I'm wondering is, how did someone slip up around here and let you run up that much credit? I've just double-checked with your bank. You got a double zero *there,* anyway." He chortled mirthlessly and it sounded like the rumble of a wildcat's snarl. "We got a problem, don't we? How do we get our ten G's back?"

"You'll get it back!" I snapped. "You should know that if I leave any unpaid markers lying around I'm all washed up in any decent-sized game or house between Nome, Alaska, and the Florida Keys!"

"Sure." He didn't sound impressed. "I'll put it another way, friend: *When* do we get it back?"

"I need a little time to get organized."

"Like the next thirty years?" he sneered. "I got another problem, even, a real impatient partner who wants to talk about it right now, friend!"

"You can tell your impatient partner the same thing I just told you—friend!" I said icily. "I need a little time—"

"Mike, baby!" He nearly laughed in my face. "You don't think for a moment you got any choice about this?"

I took a quick glance toward the steel door that closed off the outside world so effectively; saw the air of brutal competence about the two goons standing in front of it; then looked back at Arndt and shrugged.

"I guess you're right, Walter," I told him. "So in about thirty minutes from now I'll be a soggy mess of pulp in the back alley?"

"You figure the satisfaction of having a cheap bum like you beaten up is worth ten grand?" This time he did laugh, and it didn't make for pleasant listening. "You got to be out of your mind, Farrel."

"Okay," I slid off the bar stool onto my feet. "Let's go talk with your partner. Maybe I can make a long-term deal to wash dishes, or something?"

On the far side of the room was a locked door concealed behind a thick drape, and beyond it was a maze of corridors and a couple of flights of stairs. I got lost just following Arndt, but finally we wound up in some kind of entrance hall on the top story. He knocked sharply, then went right in without waiting for an invitation. I followed him dutifully into the elegantly furnished living room of what was obviously a penthouse apartment, and wondered vaguely just how many people knew of its existence.

"This is Farrel," Walter Arndt said to the high back of an armchair. He waited until a cone of silky blonde hair rose above the chairback, then added, "Farrel, meet my partner, Arline Gray."

The blonde got to her feet and moved around the armchair to take a long penetrating stare at me. Her azure blue eyes were set wide apart in the tight mask of her heart-shaped face, and there was a sensual, but fully controlled, twist to her full mouth, accentuated by the slightly protruding lower lip. She was tall and held herself erect; her small, sharp-tipped breasts thrust horizontally against the thin silk of her white blouse, and her coral-colored shantung pants molded rounded hips and long tapering legs.

Her face, her figure, her carriage, were all very controlled. Logic said that this was a very controlled dame indeed, and maybe the closest she'd ever gotten to real passion was the window of a jewelry store. But that sensually twisted mouth was a challenge all by itself, making me wonder just how much dynamite was packed under her icy exterior, and if a guy could light the fuse, would he wind up with a damp squib or nuclear fission?

"Let's see the profile," she said suddenly, in a cool, completely impersonal voice.

"Huh?" I gaped at her for a moment.

"You heard what she said!" Arndt rasped. "Turn sideways, so Arline can get a good look."

I did as he said and it seemed a long time before she told me it was enough and I faced her again.

"A gray rinse wouldn't be any problem," she said, more to herself than anyone else. "I guess he'll do, then, Walter."

"We've been looking a long time," Arndt conceded, "and he's the best yet. We're also running out of time real fast."

"Then he'll have to do!" She smiled, showing even

white teeth, and for no good reason I wondered if a tigress ever smiled at its dinner while it was still on the hoof.

"Welcome home, Mike Kluger!" she said sweetly.

"Farrel," I corrected her. "Mike Farrel."

"That, my friend"—the sweetness abruptly vanished "was before you owed us ten thousand dollars."

"Why don't you sit down and talk it over, Mike?" Walter Arndt suggested. "Or maybe you just can't wait to get down into the alley, huh?"

chapter two

After I had studied the photograph for a long time, I looked up and met the steady gaze of Arline Gray's blue eyes. She was sitting comfortably in her high-backed chair, her hands folded in her lap, like the president of a women's club waiting for a vote of confidence without the slightest doubt in her own mind that she'll get it.

"That's the real Mike Kluger?" I said, finally breaking the long silence.

"Oh, boy!" Arndt said disgustedly. "This Farrel is one smart guy, I'm telling you!" He moved around toward the blonde's chair with sudden impatience. "Maybe I should do him a favor and throw him out the window?"

"Shut up, Walter," Arline Gray said in an even voice. "Yes, Mike, that's the real Kluger."

"He's a lot younger than me," I said.

"That picture was taken seven years back, Mike." She glanced at Walter Arndt momentarily. "I'd like a drink. Maybe Mike would, too?"

Arndt scowled at me and I told him bourbon. He moved across to the cellaret with all the indignation of a Roman gladiator the empress has somehow gotten confused with a lousy Christian.

"You figure I look enough like this Kluger to impersonate him?" I asked the blonde.

"With a gray rinse through your hair," she said, nodding. "But that's no problem. My personal hair stylist can take care of it."

"Goody!" I snarled, and the corners of her mouth quirked in acknowledgement. "So give me some good reasons why I should become this guy Kluger?"

Arndt thrust a glass into my hand, then delivered Arline's drink before he took his own to the couch, which would give him a point of vantage to act like an umpire between the two of us. He plumped down onto the upholstery and his soiled brown eyes glittered at me.

"Mike Kluger was an iceman," he grated. "Heisted a bundle of uncut diamonds from a dealer seven years back. The fuzz caught up with him but they never did catch up with the hot ice. Kluger hid it someplace and hid it real good. Nobody ever found it, not in seven long years, friend!"

"So he's been in jail these last seven years?" I queried.

"San Quentin," the blonde agreed. "He gets released in six days from now."

"Keep talking," I growled. "Somewhere down the line there's got to be something that makes sense."

"So he stashed the hot ice someplace," Arndt continued in the same grating voice. "He knew the cops were on to him and he'd get the book thrown at him when they didn't find the bundle. Kluger had to stash it away someplace real good so it'd still be there years later when he got out of the can. Our bet is he left it with somebody—his wife, maybe?"

"This gets better all the time!" I sneered. "You mean you want me to impersonate a guy to his own wife?"

"There are circumstances," Arline Gray said easily. "Mike Kluger was only married three months before he went to jail. For the last six weeks before he was caught, he was on the East Coast playing footsie with the cops while his wife was still out on the West Coast. During the whole seven years he's been in San Quentin, she saw him once a month for the first three years, then just stopped visiting him completely."

"That's right," Arndt grunted. "She hasn't seen him

in four whole years, friend, and that amount of time in the clink can change a guy a whole lot!"

"So that takes care of his wife—maybe," I said. "What about the rest of his family?"

"He's an orphan." Arline smiled dreamily. "That means no relatives at all. A guy like Mike Kluger just doesn't have friends—only business associates, and we can tell you all about them. None of them have seen him in seven years, either!"

"And I got to do all this in six days, before the real Kluger gets out of San Quentin?" I said thinly.

"Don't keep on jumping to conclusions, Mike," she snapped. "You've got six days to become Mike Kluger, then you start impersonating him!"

"Won't that make it kind of confusing for his everloving wife?" I asked. "Two husbands arriving home from seven years' jail at the same time? I can just hear her saying, 'Will the real Mike Kluger come to bed?' Are you both out of your minds?"

She sighed gently. "The real Mike Kluger will find an old friend waiting for him the moment he's released, and then find himself detained indefinitely—until the moment you're safely out of the picture with those uncut diamonds!"

"You're crazy!" I said flatly.

"We've gone to a lot of time and trouble setting this up," Arndt rasped. "It can be done, Farrel, we're sure of it. When Kluger gets home, whoever's got the ice is going to wait to be contacted—and if they don't hear from Kluger, they'll go to him! That's all you got to do, friend. Make like you're Mike Kluger, hot out of the can, then sit around and wait for somebody to bring the ice to you. When you got your mitts on it, you blow. Simple, right?"

"How much exactly is this hot ice worth?" I asked casually.

"It was insured for seventy thousand," Arline said, "but it's probably worth a lot more. The nice thing about uncut diamonds is that once you cut them, they can't be easily traced. Pick your markets and don't

unload them in a hurry—one at a time here and there
—and you can pick up the full value. No fence to
cheat you out of seventy per cent or more of their
real value!"

"What do I get out of the deal, if I go through with
it?"

"You get off the hook for ten grand, that's what!"
Arndt said savagely. "You get your markers back,
friend."

"And?" I made it sound polite.

"And think yourself goddamned lucky to get off
the hook!" he exploded.

"Shut up, Walter!" Arline smiled at him. "If Farrel
was a fool in the first place, we wouldn't be talking a
deal with him now, would we?" She switched her gaze
toward me. "As Walter said, Mike, you get your
markers back—and twenty thousand in cash."

"You're crazy!" Arndt told her.

"Practical," she corrected him. "How about it,
Mike?"

"How about there isn't any bundle of uncut diamonds anymore?" I queried. "What if whoever he
stashed them with, cut out to South America six years'
back and cashed in on them?"

"I don't think it's possible," she said evenly. "But
it's a chance we all have to take. If we find out that's
the truth, then there's nothing in it for any of us—"

"Maybe we can give him his markers back, anyway," Arndt grunted. "Like the consolation prize for
the booby."

"E for effort?" Arline gurgled lazily. "Why not?
He'll never make that ten grand to pay off what he
owes us."

"You read my mind," Walter said sourly. "Okay—
how about it, Farrel?"

"Let me think it over," I told him.

What the hell was there to think over? To protect
himself, Arndt would have to make an example of any
guy who welshed on him for ten grand. A merciless
beating in the back alley could be the least of it.

Maybe a slug in the back of my head would be his idea of justice. So I didn't have a choice, I told myself, but that was only part of it. The rest was the heady aroma of easy money in my nostrils. Twenty grand in cash and markers back, the blonde promised; it sounded attractive, but nowhere near as attractive as the thought of a bundle of uncut diamonds worth maybe a hundred grand clutched in my hot little hands!

"One more thing," I said slowly, "there won't be just Mike Kluger's ever-loving wife waiting for him to come home. The cops, and the insurance company investigators—they'll be waiting for him too, hoping he'll lead them straight to the loot!"

"That's right," Arline said. "Nobody said it's going to be easy for you, Mike. But then—nobody ever made thirty thousand dollars that easy, did they?"

"You want to chicken out, I'll almost be grateful," Arndt said softly. "Maybe I can't get ten grand out of your hide, but it'll be a pleasure just trying!"

"Stop scaring me, Walter," I told him. "I have to think this thing out."

"Take all the time you want," Arline said, smiling.

"I just did," I said, "and I'm in."

"I'm glad!" Her voice was a little warmer than it had been before. "You won't regret it, Mike."

"The thing is, I'm not too goddamned sure if I will," Arndt muttered. "Okay, so he's in."

I finished my drink, put down the glass, then stood up leisurely. "When do you want me to call around for my first lesson on how to become a Mike Kluger for fun and profit?"

"Sit down!" Walter snarled. "You're not going anyplace."

"You're staying right here, Mike," Arline said conversationally. "There's a guest room, and you can learn your lessons without anything else disturbing your concentration until it's time to leave for the West Coast!"

I sank back into my chair and lit a cigarette. Arndt

got up from the couch and slouched toward the door, a brooding look on his sallow face. He stopped when he reached it and turned back toward me.

"Get a couple of things real clear in your head, Farrel," he said in a soft voice. "Don't try and walk out of this apartment, because you won't get ten yards, and don't try and make anything out of this situation with Arline. It's strictly business, you understand that real good! I get one whisper from Arline that you even looked like you were about to step out of line, and you'll regret it! You got all that real clear?"

"Like crystal, Walter," I assured him. "Just tell me one thing before you go, to satisfy my idle curiosity."

"Like what?" he said with an impatient shrug.

"Is that roulette wheel of yours rigged?"

He smiled. "You saw it pay off seven G's to that blonde, didn't you? You think if it was gaffed we'd have given up that kind of dough?"

"Yeah. Well, that payoff to the blonde is what hooked me," I muttered sourly. "It was the biggest in six weeks. In the hole like I was, I lost my marbles when I saw it."

"I noticed," he commented. "You can almost guess when a guy who calls himself a pro is going to crack under the strain and turn into first-class schmo."

Then it hit me, like a sap on the back of the skull. "The wheel *was* gaffed. You rigged that payoff hoping I'd make a monkey of myself!" I could have cut my throat for real now.

"Like you said," he said through an ugly half-smile, "it sometimes takes a gaff to land a dumb fish!"

The door closed in back of him. I just sat there for a while appreciating the whole bit, and thinking how a girl called Julie Holland would laugh if she ever heard the story—or maybe she wouldn't laugh at all, just cry a little.

"Get me another drink, please?" the blonde asked politely.

I took her glass along with my own to the cellaret

and made fresh drinks. She studied my face with the same cold concentration she had when she first saw me, as I came back across the room toward her.

"You look an awful lot like Mike Kluger even now," she murmured, "without the prematurely gray streak in your hair. It's—it's almost unnerving!" She took the glass out of my hand, her eyes still intent on my face.

"I knew Mike Kluger a long time back, knew him real well. Before he was married, of course. I was only a kid, then, and naive enough to figure he was the most wonderful thing that had ever happened to me in my whole life! It didn't take me that long to find out just what a chromium-plated heel he really was, but by that time it was a little late." She looked away from me suddenly. "But a girl can never forget the first man who—"

She stood up quickly and moved away from me across the room, changing the subject as she went.

"It's gotten so late I'm sure you must be as tired as I am, Mike." Her voice now had the exact right intonations of the hostess tactfully trying to rid herself of the last loaded guest at the party.

"We'll start your lessons in the morning." She gestured gracefully. "Your room is this way."

The guest room was furnished the same way as the living room, its elegance enhanced by the sybaritic deep-piled white rug beside the bed and the rich, plum-colored satin cover and cushions that matched the drapes.

Arline turned toward me for the first time since she'd gotten up from the couch, and her face was a taut mask again, held under rigid control.

"I'll get Walter to send one of the boys over for your things in the morning." She smiled vaguely. "But for tonight you'll just have to rough it, I guess."

"It'll be tough," I said, taking a second look at all that satin and jazz, "but you've got a built-in survival kit in the living room if I weaken."

"You want anything from the cellaret, help yourself, of course," she said. "Good night, then?" She nodded briefly then walked out of the room.

"Good night," I told the door as it closed behind her, and wondered what the hell I'd done—or hadn't done?—to rate such an obvious brush-off.

I smoked a couple of cigarettes and then, figuring she'd had time enough to be out of the way, I went back to the cellaret and made myself a king-sized nightcap. Back in the guest room I put the drink carefully down on the bedside table, stripped off my clothes, took a quick shower to get rid of the stale odor of Arndt's crooked wheel that I felt somehow still clung to me, then slid under the satin covers.

All fairy tales are horror stories, I remembered uneasily, and didn't I have a vague childhood memory of one about an ogre who always gave his intended victim a last night of luxury—a magnificent repast followed by a night in a sumptuous bed—before he ate them, or whatever, the following day? The memory called for the nightcap, so I leaned back against the cushions, the drink in one hand and a cigarette in the other, and wondered again just exactly what I'd gotten myself into with this deal.

How about the real Mike Kluger? What was the phrase Arline Gray had used?—*He'll be detained indefinitely.* What the hell did that mean exactly? They were going to hold him prisoner someplace, or chop him into small pieces and drop them into the Pacific Ocean? And how about his wife, who hadn't seen him the last four years? Maybe she'd quit visiting him in San Quentin because she'd lost interest, and she'd split his loot with a new lover? Would that be the kind of setup waiting for me when I walked into Kluger's home? The nervously smiling wife standing in front of the picture window at the far side of the room, while behind the open door, lover-boy waited with an ax poised?

This is where you need a little philosophy, Farrel, I told myself, along with a little more booze. The blonde was damned right about one thing, so keep it in mind! Nobody ever made thirty thousand bucks easy! A split second later a soft tap on the door made my whole body jump.

"Come in?" I called out in a kind of strangled voice, expecting almost anything, from a couple of Arndt's goons, to a four-headed ogre with just the one eye dead center of the third head.

The door swung open and Arline Gray stepped inside the room, carefully closed it behind her, then came toward the bed where I sat with my tranquilizers in each hand. She'd taken her hair down, and instead of the inverted cone, now her silky blonde hair hung in rippling waves that danced sensuously with every step she took. Even the soft light from the bedside lamp was strong enough to reveal the transparency of the thin silk nightgown that only reached the middle of her thighs.

"Arline?" I sat bolt upright, put the drink down on the table, and stubbed out the butt of my cigarette. "What is it?"

She came close enough to touch me, then sat down on the bed facing me, her blue eyes suddenly enormous.

"Mike?" she whispered. "It's been so long!"

"Huh?" I grunted.

"All those years, Mike! They weren't fair!" There was a sound of urgency in her voice as she cradled my face in her hands, while her eyes searched mine with passionate intensity.

"I can't wait any longer," she said huskily. "You can understand that, can't you?"

"Huh?" I repeated blankly.

"Of course you can, darling!"

Somewhere down the line her rigid self-control had vanished completely. When her full lips clamped to mine, they trembled with wanton abandon. The tip of her tongue probed and thrust, her sharp white teeth nibbled, then savaged, my lower lip. At the height of her frenzied assault she pulled away and stared blank-

ly into my face, while her long nails dug brutally into
my bare chest.

"All those years," she said jerkily, "it was building
up inside me and I never knew until now. Understand me, Mike, please? I can't hold it back anymore.
I'm just not responsible for what I do. It's not my
fault, it's yours!"

Arline rose to her feet as she finished speaking.
Then, a moment later, she peeled off her nightgown
in a rapid, impatient movement. For a timeless moment I stared at the flawless beauty of her body;
the pointed thrust of her small breasts, their coral
tips hard with desire, the flowing harmony of curving
hips and firm shapely thighs. Then she leaned forward
and switched off the bed lamp.

"Want me, just a little, Mike!" she moaned softly
in the darkness, before she threw herself down onto
the bed. "I need you so much!"

I was the guy who came to make a deal, and stayed
to reap a whirlwind. Even when it was all over and
she lay sobbing happily in my arms, I still didn't know
why. It didn't seem like the right time to ask, exactly.

chapter three

"There, I guess that about does it!"

The hair stylist moved around to the back of my chair, then ran her fingers contemptuously across my scalp, digging her sharp nails into the tender skin as they went. Her name was Monica, and she'd arrived every morning by appointment during the last six days. She was also a little redheaded creep with an oversized bust which, coupled with a regrettable shortness of thigh, gave her a permanently top-heavy look.

"I told you before," I snarled, "don't do that!"

"Sorry, kiddo!"

She lowered her voice a fraction to make sure she wasn't overheard by Arline, who was someplace else in the penthouse.

"I figured you'd gotten so house-trained by now, you wouldn't even yelp when a girl manhandled you a little."

I turned my head and met the open sneer in her heavily mascaraed eyes. She shoved that oversized bust at me, straining her white nylon dress to bursting point, then winked heavily.

"It's all real, kiddo! Maybe I'll let you prove it. Sit up and beg real nice like you always do for Miss Gray, huh?"

"What's with you?" I asked in a strangled voice. "Whatever it is, why the hell take it out on me all the time?"

"I got to work myself into a premature old age just making a living," she whispered fiercely, "while you're

living it up in this penthouse making like a pet poo-
dle! Every time I even look at you, I get sick to my
stomach! I'd give a week's pay for the chance of getting away with one good belt across that sniveling
face of—" Her face changed its expression with mi-
raculous speed, from naked loathing, to the vacuous
simpering mask she wore normally.

"I guess that about does it!" she said in a hideously
genteel voice. "What do you think, Miss Gray?"

I looked back and saw Arline standing in the guest
room doorway watching us. She wore a very elegant
white and beige print dress, and her rigid self-control
made her look like she'd just stepped out of the pages
of a high fashion magazine.

"I think that's just fine, Monica," she said easily.
"You've done an excellent job."

"Thank you, Miss Gray!" The little creep almost
drooled, as she put her hand back on top of my head
for a moment. "I really think it makes Mr. Farrel
look even more distinguished—" her nails sank into
my scalp for the last time "—and I wouldn't have figured that was possible, would you, Miss Gray?"

"You can clean up your things and go now, Monica," Arline said coolly. "I'll express my appreciation
in a more practical way when you come for my next
appointment."

"Oh, thank you, Miss Gray!" Monica squealed ec-
statically.

"I've made you a drink in the living room, Mike,"
Arline said evenly. "You'd better hurry, it's getting
warmer by the minute." Then she turned and walked
back into the living room.

"Maybe next week," the hair stylist whispered sly-
ly, "she won't bother telling you what to do? Maybe
she'll buy you a little gold collar, and a diamond-stud-
ded leash to go with it? Then all she's got to do is pull
it, and you'll go wherever she wants, right?"

I got out of the chair and saw she was turned away
from me, leaning over the small table as she put her
hair-styling implements back into a kind of attaché

case. Monica had an oversized rump to match her oversized bust and the temptation was irresistible. I goosed her with brutal efficiency; she reacted with a frantic squeal, and a convulsive leap forward that spilled the case of equipment, the small table, and Monica herself, onto the floor in a confused heap. Her legs threshed wildly for a moment, then she rolled over and dragged herself up onto her knees and glared bloody murder at me.

"As Miss Gray won't express her appreciation until the next appointment, I figured I should express mine right now," I told her happily. "And—if you don't mind me asking—what ever happened to the top half of your legs?"

Arline had a mildly inquiring look on her face when I walked into the living room. "What was all the noise?"

"Monica had a small accident. Nothing permanent, I regret," I told her while I collected my drink from the cellaret.

"Come and sit over here, Mike." She patted the vacant space on the couch beside her. "You know, she was right. That gray rinse does give you a kind of distinguished look, at that!"

"The hell with looking distinguished," I growled, as I sat down beside her. "All I want is to look like a guy named Mike Kluger."

"You do," she said slowly, "even more so, now. It's still almost unbelievable how—" Then she stopped abruptly while a red-faced, redheaded hair stylist hurried past us with her face carefully averted.

Arline waited until she heard the outside door close —shutting out Monica from my life forever, I fervently hoped—then continued, "Are you all packed?"

"Ready and raring to go," I agreed.

She glanced at her watch. "We have a half hour before I need drive you out to the airport. Walter will be waiting for you when you get to L.A. I think maybe we should use that last thirty minutes for a quick run-through, okay?"

I shrugged. "Whatever you say."

A sideways glance at her heart-shaped face made me wonder if that controlled twist to her sensual mouth had ever relaxed into a sudden fury of passion and frenzy. After her unexpected visit the first night I'd stayed in the penthouse, she'd acted as if it had never happened. From the next morning on, our relationship had been strictly businesslike all the way down the line. Never once, by word or action—by a momentary look, even—had she made any reference to that night. It had gotten so that now I had trouble believing it myself, and it had me worried because I still didn't get it at all.

"What is your given name, Mr. Kluger?" she snapped suddenly.

"Michael Gavin Kluger," I said dutifully.

"Your wife's name?"

"Diane."

"Before you were married?"

"Diane Merton."

"Where were you married?"

"Las Vegas, July 24, 1956, a little place on the Strip, called—"

"Describe your wife, Mr. Kluger, as you remember her."

"A blonde, wearing her hair long the last time I saw her," I said automatically. "Kind of pretty, good figure—"

"I guess some of your business associates will look you up when you get home, Mr. Kluger. Like who, for instance?"

"Chris Edwards," I answered, "Lou Stern, Sonny West."

"What about George Trent?" she asked sharply.

"Who?"

"You heard me!"

I hesitated for a moment, then shook my head. "I don't know any George Trent."

"That's right." She smiled. "What was the name of the arresting officer?"

"Cromby, Lieutenant Cromby."

"What's your house number?"

"It doesn't have a number, it has a name," I said. "Something real original, too. 'Sea Breezes.' You think that makes the real Kluger some kind of a poet, Arline?"

She relaxed and leaned back against the cushions. "I guess it makes you some kind of an authority on Mike Kluger. I quit. You're letter-perfect, Mike."

"It's fine during rehearsal," I muttered. "I just hope I stay that way when the curtain goes up in front of a strictly live audience."

"You will," she said in an almost complacent voice.

"Walter will keep in touch, I guess?" I queried. "I wouldn't want to have those uncut diamonds burning a hole in my pocket while I waited around for you to contact me."

"Don't worry," she said coldly. "Walter's going to stay real close to you the whole time, Mike. Think about that when you do have the stones burning a hole in your pocket. It could stop you getting any stupid ideas about double-crossing us!"

"Arline, honey!" I looked at her reproachfully. "You mean, you don't trust me?"

"We trusted you for ten grand," she snapped, "and look where that got us?"

"There has to be an answer to that," I muttered. "Why can't I think of it?"

She looked at her watch again. "We might as well start for the airport. Your airline ticket, and a hundred for expenses, are on the table over there. Go get your bag, while I check my lipstick."

"What kind of a farewell is this—to a house guest of six whole days' duration?" I asked in a shocked voice. "It doesn't even rate as a sailor's farewell?"

"Why don't we call it a Farrel's farewell?" she said sweetly. "So—hello, Mike Kluger!"

The plane got into Los Angeles a little after five that afternoon. Walter Arndt was waiting for me in the terminal building. He grabbed my arm as I came close, and hustled me into a waiting car outside.

"Why all the rush?" I snarled, as he headed the car into the airport traffic.

"We got a couple of hours' drive ahead of us," he said shortly. "Then I'm dropping you ten miles this side of the town, and you get the bus in. Maybe somebody's watching to see Mike Kluger come home, so we'd better do it right."

"Sure," I said. "How about the real Mike Kluger? I hope he's not on his way home at the same time."

"You don't have to worry, friend," he said softly. "He's been detained—indefinitely! Give me your wallet."

"What?"

"Don't argue!"

"Okay." I dug out my wallet, carefully extracted what was left of the hundred Arline had given me, then handed it to him.

Arndt tucked it into his coat pocket. Then he dug inside his coat, pulled out another wallet, and tossed it into my lap.

"Now you're really Mike Kluger," he said easily, "and you got all the identification you need to prove it!"

It was Kluger's wallet all right. I thumbed through the contents and found nothing else besides the identification I needed. So I put my money into it, then dropped it back into my inside coat pocket.

"How was Arline when you left?" Walter asked suddenly.

"Fine, I guess," I told him. "Like usual, anyway, the only iceberg that wears a skirt I ever met in my whole life."

He chuckled. "Maybe it takes a better personality than yours to thaw out that dame, hey?"

"Who do you know?" I asked interestedly, and that finished the conversation for the next hour at least.

By the time I'd almost forgotten Arndt could talk, he broke the silence again. "The bus station's only another couple of miles," he said bleakly. "I'll call you in the morning and see how things are, right?"

"Sure," I agreed. "What happens if I want to contact you in a hurry?"

"You don't!" he said flatly. "But don't worry, I'll call you twice a day, morning and evening, from here on out."

"Won't that make my ever-loving wife a little curious?"

"So tell her I'm a guy you met in San Quentin," he grunted. "Got out a couple of weeks before you did, and I've got a hot business proposition that needs a lot of figuring out!"

"Okay." I shrugged resignedly.

He braked the car to a stop about fifty yards from the bus station. "You're on your own, Mr. Kluger," he said gently, "and I got just one word of advice. Don't blow it if you want to live to a ripe old age—like into next week?"

I got out and Arndt made a quick U-turn, heading back in the direction we'd just come from. When he was out of sight, I picked up my bag and started walking. After I'd bought a ticket I found out it was only ten minutes to bus time, and that was something—not having a long wait to put my nerves further on edge. I filled in the time by pretending I really was Mike Kluger savoring his first day's freedom after seven long years and noticing all the things that had changed in that time. Like the girls' skirts were a lot shorter, and so was their hair; I never got any further in my observations because my steady gaze must have embarrassed the blonde; she got up from her seat and took cover in back of a solid pillar.

The bus ride, and then the cab ride out to the house, took about another hour between them, so it was dark when I arrived. I paid off the cab, then walked up the drive toward the house, my heart pumping like I'd sprung about five different leaks at the same time.

It took maybe five seconds after I'd thumbed the doorbell, before the door opened and I stepped into the front hall. There was nobody to greet me, and I figured whoever had opened the door to me just hadn't had the time to vanish. The whole bit didn't help my nerves any. Then I saw, as I closed the door, that it had a remote-control gismo with wires running from it along the wall, and I felt a little better. Strong enough to follow the wires, anyway, figuring they had to lead me to whoever had operated the gismo in the first place.

The wires led me into the living room, which was in darkness. I stood in the doorway uncertainly, feeling my spine crawl as I remembered an earlier vision of Kluger's wife having found a new lover-boy. Maybe he was waiting just a few feet away in the darkness, with an ax poised ready to give me cleavage where even a dame never had cleavage before.

"Mike?" a soft, throaty voice asked from deep in the darkness.

"Who else?" I growled."

"You know where to find the switch!"

I ran my hand down the wall until I found the switch. Soft light suddenly flooded the room, and then I saw her, standing at the window with her back toward me.

"I didn't expect you for another hour yet," she said.

"I made good connections," I said, and started toward her.

When I was about six feet away, she made a small gesture of dismissal with her hand.

"No passionate reunions, Mike," she said steadily. "No loving caresses. All that died a long time back, a million years or more!"

I stopped where I was and stared numbly at her back." I guess you're right, Diane," I mumbled.

"Why did you bother coming back here?" she asked, a few seconds later.

"Don't you know?" I grated.

She shrugged listlessly. "Whatever it is has brought you back, I'm not really interested. Are you staying long?"

"It depends," I said truthfully.

"Are you hungry? There's food in the icebox."

"I've eaten," I told her, "but I sure could use a drink."

"I guess we should have a drink to celebrate your freedom," she murmured. "I owe you that much."

My nerve ends tightened again as she slowly turned around toward me. This was the first and biggest test of all. If Kluger's wife accepted me as her husband, then it was almost a certainty that anyone else who had known him before he went to jail would also accept me.

Her blonde hair was the color of ripe corn, cut short, and the hairdo was no less attractive for being strictly conventional. The slightly plump cheeks dimpled at the corners of her wide, generous mouth, while her light blue eyes had the opaque look of Venetian glass, which somehow belied their candid gaze. She wore a charcoal cotton-knit blouse that revealed the swelling curves of full deep breasts and a trim waistline. The blue skirt sat snug over hourglass hips and strong thighs. Her body had the dual appeal of the full ripeness of young womanhood, coupled with an enduring earthy strength of absolute femininity.

"Have I changed so very much in seven years?" she asked softly.

"For the better, Diane," I said carefully. "You're very beautiful."

"You always were a conscientious liar, I remember." She smiled without malice.

"How about me?" I asked. "Have I changed much?"

"You sound different, somehow," she said in a musing voice. "You almost sound a little nervous. I don't ever remember you being nervous, Mike. But then it's been a long time."

"Sure." I nodded, feeling the sweat trickling down my spine. "A long time."

"Some of your old friends haven't forgotten you, though." There was a strong trace of irony in her voice. "I thought the phone would never stop ringing today. Chris Edwards called—so did Lou Stern and Sonny West. They can't wait to see you now you're free again, and I just bet it's got nothing to do with the jewels, either!"

"They don't stand a chance!" I snarled.

"I guess you hid them someplace real good," she said idly. "For the first couple of years after you'd gone, they never stopped hounding me. Not only your old buddies like West and the others, but the police and the insurance investigators, too. They never stopped trying for those first two years, Mike! But I told you that a long time ago, didn't I." She made it a statement.

"It must have been tough for you," I said.

"I got used to it," she said flatly. "I didn't even bother telling them that when we got married I still thought you were a legitimate businessman. I guess that might have been good for a laugh, anyway. How you told me you had to go to New York on business, and the first time I realized exactly what kind of business you were in, was when I read about your arrest in the newspapers."

That did up everything just fine, I thought sourly, if Kluger's wife had figured him for an honest john right up to the time of his arrest. She would have been about the last person in the whole world he would have confided in—or trusted to keep his loot hidden from all those insurance investigators and police officers.

"How about that drink to celebrate your homecoming?" Diane Kluger asked politely.

"Oh, sure. What will you have?"

"My usual," she said complacently.

"What is your usual these days?" I asked.

"The same as always, Mike."

"I haven't tasted alcohol in seven long years." I strove to keep my voice on a casual note. "I forget what it tastes like. I even forget what your usual drink was Diane."

"Rye and ginger ale," she said promptly.

There was a small bar set in a corner of the room, and it was well equipped, with everything neatly in place. I busied myself making the drinks, giving my glass about four ounces of straight bourbon over a couple of lonely ice cubes. Then I turned around to carry the drinks back across the room, and saw Diane Kluger had moved from the window and was about to sit down in an armchair. It was a very fancy, fussy-antique chair, with wooden arms that had been elaborately carved by some ancient craftsman who must have had plenty of time and talent but no taste. The hem of her skirt caught on one of the carved projections just as she sat down, forcing the skirt to hike up her thighs.

I got about halfway across the room toward her, then stopped suddenly. She was sitting in the chair with her arms crossed under her breasts, her face completely composed, her whole body relaxed. The fact that her skirt was hiked up to the very tops of her thighs—revealing the whole length of her shapely legs, her garters, and the delicate black fringe of her panties —obviously didn't worry her at all. What the hell was she trying to do exactly? I wondered. If it was meant to be seductive, then why did nothing else about her attitude jibe with that intimate exposure of her legs? About the last word to describe her facial expression was provocative. It didn't make any sense.

"Mike?" She looked steadily at the wall opposite. "Is something wrong?"

Then a couple of minor details came together in my mind. The remote-control gismo on the front door; the hall was well-lit when I arrived but the living room had been in darkness.

"You have very beautiful legs, Diane," I told her.

"Thank you." She didn't sound enchanted at the compliment.

"And I think those panties are real cute, with the black lace and all," I added.

Her face stiffened; then her right hand touched the naked flesh of her thigh for a brief second before it fumbled frantically, and found the projection which had caught her hem as she sat down. She hastily freed her skirt, then pulled it down to her knees, while a deep pink stained her cheeks.

"Diane," I said gently. "How long have you been blind?"

"Does it matter?" Her face turned toward the sound of my voice. "A lot longer than you've been Mike Kluger, I imagine."

chapter four

She drank some of her rye and ginger ale, then lowered the glass from her lips. "How did I know you weren't Mike Kluger?" A slow smile quirked the corners of her mouth. "The voice is different. I know Mike's voice could have changed a lot after seven years in prison, but this is something more than a change in tonal quality. Your voice has more character—more guts, I think is the right word for what I mean—than his could ever have if he lived a thousand years!"

I drank some of the bourbon because I needed it real bad right then. "I'll take a guess at just how long you've been blind," I said. "Four years?"

"How did you know?"

"You stopped visiting Kluger in prison about that time."

"You're right," she said, nodding. "He never had any of my sympathy for what he did, and I didn't want any of his. But it isn't as bad as all that. I've had two operations already, and the third is due in a couple of weeks. If it's successful I'll see again."

"That's great!" I told her.

"We'll know about that after the operation." She smiled again. "You're very adept at changing the subject, aren't you? What's your real name?"

"Mike Farrel."

"Why did you pretend to be my husband? No, that's a stupid question! You hoped I had the jewels, of course?"

"That's right," I agreed.

"You can't be a police officer. It's not the kind of thing they would do. Are you one of the insurance investigators?"

"No," I said flatly.

"One of Mike's old friends, maybe?"

"I never heard of Mike Kluger until a week back," I said.

"Then it was somebody else's idea? You must look a lot like him, if they thought you had a chance of even fooling his wife?"

"I guess I do," I said awkwardly. "They figured there was a chance of fooling you. They knew you hadn't seen him the last four years. But they didn't know you were blind."

"You wouldn't have come here if you weren't sure there wasn't a chance of my husband arriving about the same time," she said slowly. "What's happened to him?"

"He's been indefinitely detained," I answered.

The front doorbell sounded, making me spill good liquor from my glass onto the rug.

"I want to talk some more, Mike Farrel," Diane Kluger said calmly, "so maybe it would be better if you still pretend to be my husband until whoever is at the door has gone."

"Okay."

"Would you please answer it, then?"

A tall, lean character stood on the front porch, a cigarette dangling from the corner of his mouth. I opened the front door a little wider so more light from the hall spilled onto his face. He didn't fit any of the three business associates of Kluger's, whose physical descriptions were blueprinted on my mind. I was sure of that.

"What do you want?" I asked abruptly.

"You're Mike Kluger?" His voice had an irritating nasal drawl that sounded more like a whine.

"Sure, I'm Kluger," I rasped. "Who are you?"

"Name of Halloran," he said. "Global Insurance. I want a couple of minutes of your time."

"Maybe you'd better come in," I said, shrugging.

In the brighter light of the living room, Halloran didn't improve any on second inspection. He was in his mid-thirties, with thin blond hair he wore a little too long to try and hide the fact it was receding fast. His face was thin, almost gaunt, with a sharp-pointed nose and a thin mouth. His eyes were dark and kept moving the whole time, like they weren't interested in what they could see already, but had to find out what was being deliberately hidden from them.

"This is my wife." I gestured toward Diane. "This is Mr. Halloran, from the insurance company, honey."

"I've met Mr. Halloran before," she said in a pleasant voice. "He's been around quite a few times lately."

"Nice seeing you again, Mrs. Kluger," Halloran said curtly. "Just dropped in to talk to your husband for a couple of minutes."

"Go right ahead," she said lightly. "Mike and I don't have any secrets from each other."

"Fine." He looked at me for a few seconds. "Aren't you going to ask me to sit down, Kluger?"

"No," I told him.

"Okay, I'll come right to the point. My company paid out seventy thousand dollars on the claim for those diamonds you heisted and they didn't like it. They'd like to recover those stones and now you're a free man, they figure maybe they've got a better chance of doing it. Anybody who gives us information leading to the recovery of the jewels is entitled to ten per cent of the claim value, as a reward. My company's making a special exception in this case, they're offering a twenty-thousand-dollar reward for the recovery."

"It sounds like your company is getting a little desperate, Mr. Halloran." I grinned at him.

"Let me put it in words of one syllable, Kluger," he said coldly. "Turn over the stones to us, we'll give you a check for twenty thousand, and you're clean. Try and get rid of them any other way and the law jumps you for handling stolen goods. That way you go straight back to the pen, with nothing for your trouble but more time to serve in San Quentin!"

"It sounds a real good deal, Mr. Halloran." I waited long enough for his eyes to glitter eagerly, then shook my head. "I only wish I had those stones so I could get that big fat check from you right now—but I don't."

"Sure," he said savagely. "Well, if you change your mind you can always reach me through this number." He took a card from his wallet and gave it to me.

"I told you, I don't know what happened to those diamonds," I repeated.

"You told me." He glared at me for a moment. "I'd still think it over if I were you, Kluger. Right now you're a marked man and not only by the police, and me. All the easy money boys figure that, sooner or later, you got to lead them straight to a fortune in diamonds for any guy who knows how to handle them right. And once you lead them to it, they've got only one further problem—you! A lot of guys have been murdered for a tenth of what those diamonds are worth, Kluger. You ever think about that?"

"Your two minutes just ran out, Halloran," I told him. "I'll walk you to the door."

He stepped off the front porch a moment later, then hesitated for a moment. "Look, Kluger!" His voice had a pleading note which made the whining sound even more nauseous. "Don't be a sucker, huh? You don't have a hope in hell of ever picking up those rocks without there being somebody looking over your shoulder."

"You want to sell me some insurance?" I sneered.

"All right," he grated. "Just pray that it's me, or a cop, looking over your shoulder when the time comes, that's all!"

I closed the door and went back into the living room. Diane had a thoughtful expression on her face as she looked toward the sound of my footsteps.

"Maybe he's right, Mike Farrel," she said quietly. "I don't think any of my husband's so-called friends would worry about how they got their hands on those diamonds, just so long as they did. I wonder if you took on a much bigger risk than you realized, when you agreed to impersonate him?"

The door bell sounded again, like it was punctuating her words.

"Who the hell is this?" I snarled edgily.

"My guess is it's one of those so-called friends," she said, and that trace of irony was back in her voice. "Why don't you go find out?"

The moment I opened the door I knew she was right. The guy with a big grin standing there was massively built, like a heavyweight wrestler. His bushy gray hair bristled in spite of its crewcut, and his gelid gray eyes stared at me from either side of a thick fleshy nose. My memorized blueprint said this one was Chris Edwards, for sure.

"Mike baby!" He crowded into the hall, pumping my right hand up and down vigorously like he figured on detaching it from my wrist. "You look great, real great!"

"Hi, Chris."

"Wonderful to see you, baby!" He put one arm around my shoulders in a bear hug. "I guess it needs something a lot tougher than San Quentin to worry little old Mike Kluger, right? How's your wife, huh?"

"Diane's fine," I gurgled. "Come on in."

We got to the center of the living room before he finally let go of me. He beamed at Diane.

"Hi, there, Mrs. Kluger!" he boomed. "How does it feel having a husband around the house again? Real great, I bet! Only thing is you got to be careful now when the milkman comes around, right?" His thunderous guffaws drowned out the cold silence from Diane and myself.

"You want a drink, Chris?" I asked wearily.

"Don't fuss, baby, this is your big night!" He covered the distance between himself and the bar in three gigantic strides. "I can fix myself a little drink. You sit down and take it easy, boy, you got it coming!"

The phone rang and Diane lifted her head a fraction. "Get that, will you, Mike?" she asked easily.

I went across to the phone, lifted it, and said, "Hello?"

"Mike?" a thin voice asked.

"Sure, who's this?"

"Lou Stern here. Good to hear your voice again after all this time, Mike." The voice developed an enthusiastic wheeze. "I got Sonny with me right now. We figured on dropping over for a couple of minutes and say welcome home, old buddy."

"Why not?" I grunted.

"Okay, Mike, old buddy!" he wheezed emotionally. "We'll be right there. Ten minutes, at most!"

I hung up, and saw Chris Edwards watching me intently from the bar.

"Lou Stern," I told him. "Him and Sonny West are on their way over right now."

"How nice," Diane said in a level voice.

"Yeah." Chris brought his drink back to the center of the room with him, a look of open annoyance on his face. "Mike, I got to tell you one thing," he said in a confidential roar. "You don't want to trust them two bums. They pulled some real stinking deals lately! I wouldn't give them the time of day, never mind any ideas about what you're planning on with the ice, right?"

"What ice?" I grunted.

"That's the boy!" He guffawed again happily. "I should've known little old Mike Kluger was never stupid, hey?"

"That's why he's just completed seven years in San Quentin," Diane said idly.

"Hey!" Chris nudged me in the ribs with his elbow, nearly knocking me clean off my feet. "How about that? The little woman's got a real cute sense of humor, huh?"

"Is that what you call it?" I asked in a bleak voice.

It seemed no time at all before the doorbell went again, and I ushered the two callers into the living room. Lou Stern was a wizened-up little guy in his late fifties maybe, who looked something like an ex-jockey who'd lost weight. His bald head gleamed under the light, and his wrinkled skin was drawn tight across the bones of his face, giving him an unpleasant cadaverous appearance. If he ever walked into a morgue at night without being announced, the attendant would quit his job within five seconds of meeting Lou Stern.

Sonny West was a much younger guy, twenty-seven or -eight, around medium height and weight. He had had crisp, curly black hair, and somebody should have told him about using that greasy kid's stuff, but maybe they looked at his face first and changed their minds. His eyes were a dark brown and shone dully with what looked uncomfortably like an absolute hatred and contempt for the whole world. He could have been a good-looking guy, in spite of the white face and eyes, but the arrogant twist of his mouth added an open touch of sadism to his expression which was repellent. I figured Sonny was a good guy to keep away from on a bright shining day, never mind a cold dark night.

There was a whole round of greetings and back-slapping; I got them sat down, being careful none of them was real close to Diane, then made them drinks. A babble of sound continued through the whole bit of the social amenities, right up to the time when I sat down myself with a fresh drink in my hand. Then the noise suddenly vanished, like the orchestra had struck a chord and there was that momentary hush before the curtain went up.

The silence lasted a little while longer, then Lou Stern cleared his throat self-consciously. "You was unlucky, Mike," he said in a sympathetic wheeze. "Dead unlucky, old buddy! I always said that—Mike, he was dead unlucky! Didn't I say that, Sonny?" He looked at West for confirmation.

"So many times, I got tired listening to it," Sonny said in a flat voice. "You don't want to be unlucky a second time, Kluger. That way, it would figure you was just stupid."

"How do you mean that?" I asked him.

"We can handle that hot ice for you," he said. "We got the contacts and we get the right price. Nice and easy. No problems for anybody. You get your cut, we get ours."

"You can bank on one thing, Mike baby," Chris Edwards roared. "You hand them those rocks and that's the last time you see both of them for the rest of your life!"

"You want to do it right, Mike," Lou Stern wheezed anxiously. "We got good contacts—the best!"

"Listen to him, will you?" Chris raised his eyes to the ceiling, which figured to be the wrong direction if he was appealing to any higher authority. "Contacts, he says! A couple of penny-ante grifters like them couldn't handle a hot ice cream cone!"

"You got a big mouth, Edwards," Sonny West said softly, "and you keep running off at it the whole time. It don't make you sound any different from exactly what you are—a has-been heist man gone to fat!"

Edwards' huge frame trembled violently for a moment, then he managed to fight down his fury and smile at me. "Mike," he said thickly, "don't listen to the little punk. I can handle that deal for you real smooth and get twice their best price on it. And I'll still be right here to pay you off after the deal's made!"

"I like Chris, you know that, Mike?" Lou Stern wheezed breathlessly. "He's a great big likable fat slob, right? But for him to handle a deal like this?" He shook his head slowly. "It's like asking him to run for president."

"Listen, you shriveled-up old son of a pimp!" Chris thundered. "You say just one—"

"Hey!" Sonny's flat voice chopped him off in mid-sentence. "Watch your manners, you fat slob, there's a lady present."

"Don't worry about me, boys," Diane said easily. "After all, it's only my house."

"Look!" I said quickly, before they started breaking up the furniture. "I just got home maybe an hour back

—after seven years! It's great seeing you boys again, but how about giving me a break now?"

"He's right," Sonny said briskly. "We should beat it and leave the guy alone with his ever-loving." A dirty sneer showed briefly in his eyes. "After seven long years in the can, maybe a guy could've forgotten what dames are all about, even?" He got up onto his feet. "See you around, Mike. When you're ready we'll pick it up about where you left off. The town has changed a lot since the last time you saw it."

"Be a real privilege, showing you what makes it tick right now," Low Stern wheezed. "You call us whenever you're ready, old buddy, and don't forget if you want anything, any time—you just call me."

"Be seeing you, Mike baby!" An outsize fist squeezed my hand unmercifully, then pumped it up and down. "Just you don't forget one thing, boy! Chris Edwards is the guy to get you the right price for those rocks, and the guy who'll still be around to make the payoff afterwards."

It took the best part of ten minutes to hustle them out of the house and I felt exhausted by the time I got back inside the living room again.

"Make yourself another drink," Diane suggested. "I bet you need it after that."

"You're so right," I agreed, and went across to the bar. "They were Mike Kluger's friends—for real?" I said slowly a few moments later.

"So they say." She shrugged. "I never heard of any of them until the last few weeks, when they started calling me to find out exactly when my husband would be coming home. What do you think of them, Mike Farrel?"

"A bunch of creeps!" I said, then took another look at her tranquil face. "What did you think of them?"

"Collectively, the same as you," she answered slowly. "But individually there is a lot of difference between the three. Edwards sounds exactly the way West described him—a heist man gone to fat. What's a heist man? Some kind of thief?"

"A hold-up man," I explained.

"If Lou Stern ever had a prime period, he sounds like he's long past it now," she continued. "The one I'd worry about, if I had to, would be Sonny West. He sounds dangerous to me."

"He also looks dangerous," I said feelingly. "He's out to even the score with the whole goddamned world!"

"Then if you're about to continue impersonating my husband, Sonny West is the one you have to watch out for the hardest," she said quietly. "Sonny West and that insurance man, Halloran, that is. They would make a beautiful partnership." She shuddered faintly. "The scorpion and the snake!"

"You get all this from just listening to their voices?" I asked curiously.

"You lose one sense, you have to develop another." She laughed softly. "That's trite but true! I picked you as a fake from hearing your voice, didn't I?"

"That's true enough," I admitted. Then I said, "What was it you had on your mind to talk about—just when Halloran came in and you told me to stick around and keep up the act, I mean?"

"I want to hear the whole story of exactly how you got into this in the first place, Mike Farrel. I'm intrigued to know who your friends are, that they know so much about Mike Kluger, his friends, and me."

I took a chair facing her and lit a cigarette, then told the whole story, from the night I lost my last thousand bucks on the roulette wheel, up until the time I arrived at her house.

"What does this Arline Gray look like?" she asked, when I'd finished telling the story.

"A blonde," I said. "A little taller than you, and thinner, but a good figure all the same. Very controlled the whole time. A classy dresser, and I guess there's a fine razor-sharp mind tucked in back of that tight mask she wears for a face."

"How about Walter Arndt?"

"Strictly the hoodlum type, but he's managed to glue

a veneer on the outside that keeps people from rec-
ognizing what he is at first sight."

"Do they frighten you, Mike Farrel?" she asked suddenly.

"Not right here, they don't," I answered honestly.
"When they had me boxed up in that building,
with maybe half a dozen goons on tap, they frightened
me."

"I've never heard of either of them," she murmured, "and I'm sure my husband never mentioned
them before he went to prison. "She stood up, then
slowly cocked her head to one side. "Mike Farrel?"

"Yes?" I answered.

She pointed her face toward me like a hunting dog
for a moment, then walked across to my chair and
stopped maybe two feet away. "Stand up, please."

"Sure." I got onto my feet.

Her right hand lightly touched my forehead, then
her fingers explored my face. "You've heard so many
deals offered you already tonight," she said, "can you
bear to listen to just one more?"

"Why not?" I shrugged. "What can I lose now?"

"I want to know more about these two people I've
never heard of before, who know so much about my
husband and me," she said in a suddenly cold voice.
"If I send you away now, I never will, so this is my
offer of a deal. You keep right on impersonating my
husband, and I'll keep right on supporting you by pretending I believe it. In return, you tell me exactly
what happens all along the line. I want to know every
detail, what people say, and what they do. Is it a deal?"

"Sure, it's a deal. I should get so lucky after you
picked me for a fake in the first ten minutes!" I said
gratefully. "But there's one point we should clear up
right now. Supposing I get my hands on those diamonds? What then?"

"You do whatever you want with them when the
time comes," she said softly. "I'm not interested in
them. I never have been during the last seven years,
and I see no reason to change my mind now."

"What about the real Kluger?" I queried. "My friends have detained him—to use their phrase. Don't you care what happens to him in all this?"

"If it had been my husband who walked in here tonight, instead of you," she said in a low voice, "I would have told him all I wanted from him was a divorce. He tricked me into marrying him, and it was no kind of marriage in the six weeks we more or less had together before he went to New York. In all the time he's been in prison he never gave me a penny. The first two years I supported myself and kept this house going by working in my old job as a fashion consultant. Then an uncle died and left me an income wrapped up in a trust fund so I didn't need to keep on working, but I did anyway, until my eyes got so bad I had to give up."

Diane turned her head away and laughed tremulously. "You think somebody like Mike Kluger would bother coming back here just because of a woman? The only thing that could bring him back would be those diamonds! He never once gave a damn about what happened to me, and now I feel exactly the same way about him. I want to make that very clear so you fully understand my feelings, Mike Farrel, because after this the subject is closed!"

"I understand," I told her. "The subject is now closed, and we have a deal."

The phone rang again, my nerve ends jangled again, and Diane Kluger laughed again.

"It looks like it's your busy night," she said.

A woman's voice sounded nervous in my ear when I answered the phone.

"Is that you, Mike?" She sounded like she'd break apart if I told her it wasn't.

"Sure," I said guardedly.

"Oh, my God! It's so wonderful to hear your voice again, darling! Is it safe to talk?"

"Sure," I repeated blankly.

"I have to see you! Can you get away tonight—now?"

"I guess so."

"You don't know how long I've dreamed about this."
Her voice broke. "And now it's for real, I don't dare
believe it, darling! I have a ninety-minute break coming up soon. How about I meet you in Hagan's Bar in,
say, thirty minutes from now?"

"Fine," I said weakly.

"See you, lover!" she whispered, then hung up.

I stared hopelessly at the phone in my hand for a
moment before I put it down. There was no problem
—I had to meet some dame who was crazy for Mike
Kluger and flipping at the very thought of seeing him
again face to face, and I had to meet her in a place
called Hagan's Bar. It was all perfectly simple except
for a couple of small details, like I didn't know who
she was, her name, or what she looked like! Right
then seemed like a good time to go stark raving mad.

"An interesting call, Mike Farrel?" Diane asked.

I repeated the call verbatim, and voiced the obvious
problems.

"You might get your hands on those diamonds a lot
quicker than you think," she said eagerly. "If my husband left them with anyone, it would be another
woman, of course! The police lieutenant who bothered
me such a lot after his arrest swore that he'd made
a secret twenty-four-hour visit back here only two
days before they picked him up in New York. The
lieutenant was convinced my husband had come back
to see me, naturally, and I knew he hadn't, so I was
convinced the lieutenant had just invented the story to
try and frighten me!"

"So I'll go find out," I said. "But how the hell do I
pick out which one is her in Hagan's Bar? By radar?"

"You shouldn't have too much trouble," she said,
with a tinge of bitterness in her voice. "My husband
had good taste in women. You can't go wrong if you
pick the most attractive-looking woman in the place,
as long as she also looks vulnerable!"

"Wish me luck?" I said.

"I can do something a little more practical for you,

Mike Farrel." She smiled vaguely in my direction.
"There's a desk in the hall. You'll find a door key in
the drawer, and also a gun."

"A gun?"

"I got it for protection when my eyes started acting
up," she explained. "I thought that a woman living
alone, and having trouble with her vision, needed some
kind of protection. It was only an hysterical reaction
to a situation, of course. What use is a gun to a person who couldn't see what they were aiming at, anyway? But take it with you, and I'll keep my fingers
crossed that you never need it."

"Thanks a lot," I told her. "I guess I'd better get
going. See you later, huh?"

I got as far as the door leading into the hall, when
she called, "Mike Farrel?" in a different sounding tone
of voice—one I'd never heard before—that sounded
as if she was suddenly shy.

"Diane?" I stopped and looked back at her.

"You remember when you said my legs were beautiful? Was that just part of the gimmick to find out
whether I was blind, or did you mean it?"

"You have very beautiful legs," I said sincerely.

"Thank you." She flushed a deep pink, and clasped
her hands tight together in front of her, "I know it's
a dreadful thing to do to you, Mike Farrel, but—how
about the rest?"

"The rest?" I said dumbly.

"The rest of me." She giggled nervously like some
teen-age kid out on her first date. "I mean, what's
your reaction to the rest of me, apart from my legs?"

"You are an immensely attractive woman, Diane," I
told her, "and your husband must be out of his mind to
even think of passing you up."

"How do I compare with that—what was her name?
—Arline Gray, for example?" she persisted.

"If I was given the choice," I said slowly, "I
wouldn't give her another thought."

"Thank you, again." She felt quickly behind her for

the chair I'd recently vacated, then sat down, and leaned back her head with a tired look on her face.

"I'll let you go now, and I'm sorry for putting you through that ordeal." A faintly wistful quality crept into her voice. "Only it's been four years now since I've been able to look into a mirror, and after all that long a time, a girl just can't help wondering."

chapter five

It lacked ten minutes to midnight when I walked into Hagan's Bar, with that strictly nervous feeling back in the pit of my stomach again. There were a couple of guys at one end of the bar; a middle-aged lothario with a sleazy-looking blonde in the middle, and close to me was a loner, who looked like he was working his way through his tenth whisky maybe. So that left the booths against the far wall.

The first two were empty. An elderly woman sat alone quietly drinking herself into oblivion in the third. The fourth contained a young foursome, who were obviously out on a double date that looked about to collapse at any moment. The next two were empty, and the seventh contained an anxious-looking blonde with an elaborate upswept hairdo held rigid by a heavy coating of hair spray.

An unbuttoned raincoat showed a low-cut, glittering gold lamé dress underneath. Her makeup was too heavy even for a dimly lit bar at midnight.

"Sit down, Mike," she said in a taut whisper, "and just let me look at you!"

I slid into the seat opposite her and lit a cigarette, conscious of her eyes boring into me. It was the bartender who finally broke the tension; I ordered bourbon, then looked inquiringly at the girl. She gave a brief shake of her head, her gaze not wavering for a moment from my face.

"You look like you've just seen a ghost, or something." I grinned nervously at her.

"Oh, Mike!" Her eyes suddenly brimmed with tears. "It's been seven years!"

The bartender served my bourbon, then wandered back to the bar. "Here's to us," I mumbled and drank about half the contents of the glass in one gulp.

"I don't know why I'm acting so goddamned stupid," the blonde said in a half-defiant voice. "Give me a cigarette, will you?"

After I had lighted it for her, she blinked quickly a couple of times, then forced herself to lean back from the tabletop, away from me.

"You haven't changed much, Mike." Her voice was carefully casual. "Your voice is kind of different, and you look a little older, is all. I guess we all do."

I dared to take a real good look at her face for the first time. There's a certain type of skinny dame who can look real pretty, in a saccharine way, when they're very young, but they lose all pretense to any kind of looks by the time they reach thirty. This one didn't have far to go, either. Already, her face was much too thin so you couldn't help noticing her bony nose and how the corners of her narrow mouth were drawn tight into a downward curve. The heavy makeup made a kind of grotesque mask over the pale, drawn skin beneath.

"You look just fine, kid," I said warmly, "real great!"

"I'm not a kid anymore," she said fiercely. "Maybe I was the last time you saw me, Mike, but not now. It was you who made me a woman that night, or don't you even remember?"

"Sure I remember," I told her quickly. "You've hardly changed at all, honey."

"You're a lousy liar," she snapped. "Seven whole years—and not even one stinking postcard—not one miserable little word from you. I must have been crazy to believe what you said for all this time!"

"I'm glad you did believe it," I said, matching the fierceness in her voice and frantically wondering what the hell we were talking about at the same time.

" 'Wait for me,' you said, 'however long it takes you got to wait for me, because I'll be back!' That's what you said, Mike, and I was stupid enough to believe every word."

"I'm back, aren't I?"

"Yeah, you're back." She blew a thin stream of smoke toward me. "But you went home to your wife first, didn't you? And it was me who had to call you!"

"How did I know where to find you?" I let a sullen note creep into my voice. "I came right after you called, didn't I?"

"I guess you did." Her voice softened. "I'm sorry, Mike, don't get mad at me, promise?"

"Okay," I said grudgingly, "but I've been in the pen for those seven goddamn years you been waiting, don't ever forget that! You figure I wanted to be there, rather than be with you?"

"I forgot for a moment, Mike." She reached across the tabletop and gripped my forearm urgently. "I'm sorry, honest I am! Please say you'll forget it?—pretty please?"

"So forget it," I grated. "Tell me what else is new?"

"It's just that when I get to thinking about that wife of yours, I kind of flip," she said, then looked anxiously for my reaction. "You know, when I remember how it was with the two of them?"

I stared at her coldly. "You're cracking up, or something. I only ever had the one wife!"

She giggled momentarily. "You know what I mean, Mike? First you were crazy about the other one, and you got so mad when she dumped you and went off with the other guy, you turned around and married her sister before you knew what you were doing, even!"

"So a guy does a couple of stupid things in his life?" I shrugged irritably. "What does that make him in your book?"

"I'm just jealous of her, that's all." She swallowed hard, then her face slowly brightened up again. "But it was me brought you back all the way from New York, just for that one day, wasn't it?" She closed her eyes for a moment. "That was the best day I ever had in my whole life, before or since, Mike. I still remember every minute of it—every second! You knew you didn't have hardly any time left before the cops nailed you, but you took all the risk of coming back here just to be with me—for that one beautiful day!"

Her eyes were swimming again when she opened them. "Remember that drive we had in the morning out to the beach, and how you said we couldn't stay there long because the sight of me in a swimsuit would drive you clear out of your mind? We had that big lunch in the classy restaurant on the way back? It was the first time I ever tasted champagne!

"Then you took me to the amusement park in the afternoon, and spent around twenty dollars shooting at those bouncing balls on water jets, just to win me a prize to add to my collection? And that night, Mike, I was scared stiff walking into the hotel and registering as Mrs. White. Remember how I got the giggles when you told the desk clerk that was our name?"

"Sure." I nodded. "It was quite a day."

"It was quite a night, too," she said in a soft voice. "I never knew before that making love could be that wonderful. I figured I'd die with the ecstasy of it, Mike, and I didn't even care!"

"I guess I felt the same way, kid," I said huskily, and refused to think about the chances of my stomach revolting against the sickening mush that came out of my mouth.

"I've been waiting for it to happen for such a long time, Mike," she whispered. "Dreaming of the time when I'd see you again and now you're here, sitting right opposite me in this crummy bar. Tell me now— will it ever be like it was for us that night, again?"

"You know it will." I looked soulfully into her eyes. "Why else would I be here?"

She glanced at the clock over the bar, then smiled at me in a lavish token of surrender. "I have to go in a minute, darling."

The fancy hairdo and the heavy makeup, the jazzy dress underneath her raincoat; the phone conversation where she'd said she had a ninety-minute break coming up; from all that, even an idiot could figure out she was in show business. But what, exactly, was she in show business?

"Where are you working now, kid?" I asked easily.

"The Blue Goose," she said. "I was working the L.A. circuit but when I knew you were getting out, I fixed it so I'd be right here when you came back." She hesitated for a moment. "I'm through for the night about two-thirty. Will I see you after the show?"

"You bet!" I told her. "Just one thing before you go, honey. Talking about that real great day we had, you still got the package I told you to keep for me, maybe?"

Her eyes were completely blank. "You never gave me any package, Mike!"

"No?" I stared at her blank face for a while, then grinned stupidly. "You don't even remember the package, huh? The one I gave you, with all my love wrapped tight inside it, to keep until I got back?"

"Oh, Mike!" Her eyes flooded again. "You'll have me bawling my head off in front of all the customers and Mr. Edwards wouldn't like that at all!"

"Chris Edwards?" I queried.

"Sure." She looked at me curiously for a moment. "He still owns the joint."

"I figured he could have sold out," I said. "Okay, honey, you'd better not keep him, or his customers, waiting. See you right after the show."

"I took a little apartment for the time I'm working here, Mike," she murmured eagerly. "It's real nice, kind of homey even. I know you're going to like it!"

After she'd left, I signaled the bartender for another drink, and checked my watch. It was a little after twelve-thirty, so I was in no hurry to get to the Blue Goose, that was sure. The bartender delivered my fresh drink and I was about to taste it, when company slid into the seat, which must have been still warm, opposite me.

He was a thick-set guy with hard eyes, and short-cut brown hair. There was a deliberate precision in the way he took off his hat and put it down onto the tabletop that identified him as a cop maybe quicker than anything else could have.

"Having fun, Kluger?" he asked in a cold voice.

"Any reason I shouldn't?" I asked.

"None at all," he rasped. "I'm surprised you don't remember me."

"Who could forget a face like yours, Lieutenant?" I grinned nastily at him. A detailed physical description of Lieutenant Cromby, the guy who'd arrested Kluger in New York and brought him back to the West Coast to stand trial, was the last one in the set of identification blueprints I carried in my mind.

"Busy planning a new life, Kluger?" he asked abruptly. "Tell me about it. I've got a bleeding heart for an ex-con like you. I stay awake nights worrying about the guy who's paid his debt to society, getting his chance to make an honest living once he gets out."

"You've got a lousy sense of humor, too, Lieutenant," I told him.

"I stayed awake tonight wondering if you're thinking about going into the ice business?" he added, as if I hadn't even spoken. "How about that?"

"I gave up the idea," I said seriously, "I figured guys like you wouldn't even give me a chance to get started in that kind of business, Lieutenant."

He leaned against the back of the booth and raised a finger to the bartender. "Turn them over to us, Kluger," he said softly. "You're smart enough to earn an honest living—too smart to buy a return ticket to San Quentin!"

The bartender served him a small beer, and Cromby stared down at it fiercely, as if it had just said something rude about all cops, with a special reference to lieutenants.

"All you got to do is put your hands on those diamonds and—bingo!—like you're back in the clink, buddy-boy," he said crisply.

"What makes you so goddamned sure I never peddled that ice before you caught up with me?" I snarled at him. "How do you know I don't have a fat bank balance waiting for me in South America?"

"Because you didn't go to South America, you came back here," he answered smugly.

"Maybe I only came back to say my goodbyes to a couple of friends?"

"If you'd unloaded that ice, we would have known about it," he said confidently. "Nobody could have unloaded that many stones in a hurry without somebody tipping us off. No, buddy-boy, you came back to collect the loot, and the moment you do it, we'll collect you again."

He drank some of his beer, then looked at me again with a questioning stare. "Seen your wife yet, Kluger?"

"Sure." I nodded. "She's just fine."

"Did she—uh—tell you about what happened?" His voice was almost embarrassed.

"That she lost her sight, you mean?" I grunted. "Sure, she told me."

"I don't know how you ever conned a fine woman like her into marrying a punk like you," he snarled. "You got the stinking gall to sit there and tell me that after doing a seven-year stretch, you got home and found out your wife was blind, so you walked out on her again, to meet that cheap little broad who was sitting here just five minutes back?"

"You've given me a whole bunch of advice I never asked for, Cromby," I snarled back at him. "So now I'll give you some advice. Mind your own goddamned business!"

For a moment the blind fury in his eyes said he was about to bust me in the mouth, and I sat tensed, waiting for his move. Then he reached for his hat with an exaggerated, deliberately slow movement of his arm.

"You're right, buddy-boy," he said in a low voice. "My advice was lousy. You go collect your loot, and take a gun with you in case of any trouble, so if there happens to be a cop close behind you—" he gave me a death's-head grin "—why, you pull the gun on him, buddy-boy!" He climbed slowly to his feet.

"Lieutenant," I said idly, "you didn't finish your beer."

"I got to talk to the bartender about getting his drains fixed," he said coldly. "There's a stinking smell in this booth, enough to turn a real man's stomach!"

A blue neon sign spelled out BLUE GOOSE, and underneath it was a billboard with a head-and-shoulders portrait of the skinny blonde. *Janice O'Brien sings here every nite!* it said in big black print across the bottom of the picture, and I appreciated every word of it, especially the first two.

I got an alcove table and the waiter apologized when he explained I was five minutes too late for their last show. I told him a drink and a club sandwich would soothe me real fast.

By the time I was about through with the sandwich, a massive figure suddenly bulked in front of me, cutting off my view of the rest of the room.

"Mike, baby!" Chris Edwards roared. "Why didn't you say you were stepping out tonight? Can't an old friend take a little trouble to make sure you get nothing but the best?"

"It was a sudden impulse, Chris," I told him. "I got kind of restless at the house, and stepped out."

He thumped down on the cushions beside me and gestured to the waiter. "This has got to be a real celebration, boy!" He turned toward the waiter. "Get us a bottle of that imported champagne—the best!—and move it!"

The waiter disappeared so fast, I waited to see the flash of blue smoke. Edwards beamed at me fatuously. "A real celebration, huh? Just like old times and— Hey! Talking of old times I got some news that'll kill you, baby. There's an old flame of yours working right here in the club. How about that for a coincidence? Janice O'Brien singing here for the first time in seven years and who should walk in but—"

His bleak gray eyes showed the sudden calculation. "Maybe it isn't a coincidence, Mike? Maybe she's the reason you come in here, right?"

"I'm renewing old acquaintance all over tonight, Chris," I said easily. "Just had a real friendly chat with a certain Lieutenant Cromby."

"That miserable son of a bitch!" he said disgustedly. "I wonder he's lived so long."

The waiter reappeared with the champagne, opened it with a flourish, then filled two glasses.

"Here's to you, boy!" Chris lifted his glass. "Here's hoping you'll be around for a long time to come."

"I'll drink to that," I told him. "But you make it sound like the odds are against it?"

He knuckled his fleshy nose for a moment. "You know the answer to that, Mike baby. While you're sitting on that hot ice, your life just isn't worth a plugged nickel!"

"You figure I should unload it fast?"

"Well—" He shrugged massively. "Like I told you before, I got the contacts, and you know you can trust me to make the payoff, which is a hell of a lot more than you can say for Lou Stern, right?"

"I want a hundred grand—cash!" I said, trying it on for size, to see if Arline Gray had been anywhere near accurate in estimating their true worth.

"I know what you got there of course, baby," Edwards said in a dubious voice. "But—a hundred grand?"

"Uncut stones," I said crisply. "A guy takes his time and has them cut first before he unloads them— a couple here and a couple there. They'll make full market value, Chris."

"You got to pay to get them cut," he said doubtfully, "and then unloading them the way you suggest could take six months maybe, with the risk getting bigger each time you unload a single stone. I don't want to be rude, baby, but you can't afford to try it. You are hotter than a two-dollar pistol right now, Mike! The only chance you got is to pick up the stones from wherever you stashed them, and get rid of them so fast that nobody has a chance to slam their feet into your back while they're still in your hot little hand!"

"You're trying to tell me something, Chris?" I snapped.

"That kind of a deal, and the buyer gets choosy," he said almost apologetically. "He figures he's picking up a hot bundle in the first place; he's got to pay cash on the line to get them cut, and then take his chances unloading them real slow, like you said, to get full market value. He figures that kind of deal puts him in the retail business, and you in the wholesale business."

"And in the wholesale business you deal in discounts?"

"Big discounts, boy!" he rumbled. "I figure the absolute top figure you could possibly get on your own is thirty grand, because any buyer will know you're red-hot and you got to unload quick. Let me handle it, baby, and I'll guarantee you—" his eyes made a couple more quick calculations "—maybe fifty grand, and not less than forty-five!"

"Less your cut, Chris?" I reminded him.

"I'm a reasonable guy, you know that?" He blinked at me hopefully. "Let's say twenty per cent. That still leaves you way ahead on any kind of deal you could make on your own."

"I'll think about it," I told him.

"Fine," he said, nodding. "Only don't take too long, boy! I didn't like the look on Lou Stern's face tonight out at your house. He's figuring the angles, and he's a guy who always likes a short cut. With a psycho like Sonny West handling his short cuts for him, it could get real rough, Mike!" He lumbered onto his feet. "I'll go see if Janice is dressed yet, and tell her you're here."

"Thanks," I told him.

He got up and left the table. I poured myself another glass of champagne, then wondered just what the hell I had to celebrate. The way things were shaping up I'd be lucky to wind up in San Quentin doing time for the real Mike Kluger, as opposed to winding up in a gutter with a knife in my back. I refused to even contemplate my chances of getting my hands on those diamonds, because I figured they were nonexistent.

Five minutes later Janice O'Brien came up to the table with an eager smile on her face. She no longer wore the covering raincoat, and the gold lamé dress fit so tight I wondered she managed to sit down in it. For a skinny figure like hers, the tight dress was no real help, as it revealed an almost flat-breasted, boyish body, and legs that made you wonder why she was taking so long to recover from malnutrition, now she was eating right.

"Champagne?" Her voice sparkled to match the contents of the glass. "What a lovely thought, Mike!"

"Maybe," I grunted, "but it wasn't mine. It's on the house—the owner insisted."

"I wouldn't want to take any favors from Mr. Chris Edwards," she said in a dull voice. "I've taken about all I can stand from him, already."

"Then why don't we get out of here?" I suggested. "I've had about all I can drink, anyway."

The doorman found us a cab, and it dropped us outside her apartment house about ten minutes later. Janice tucked her arm in mine as we started up the stairs, hugging mine tight against her so I felt the hardness of her ribs beneath the thin flesh.

"It's on the third floor," she said softly. "I haven't got it fixed up very nice yet—I've only been in it a couple of weeks—but we won't mind, will we, Mike?" She mashed my arm some more. "I still can't believe it's true, Mike. You and me together with the rest of the night ahead of us. You just don't know how much I love you, darling, but I swear I'm going to prove it to you before it's morning!"

We reached the second floor, then started up the next flight of stairs.

"Don't get tired, lover." Janice giggled happily. "Paradise is just another nine stairs away!"

She fumbled inside her purse for the door key when we finally reached her apartment, then gave a dramatic sigh of relief when she found it.

"Imagine if I'd dropped it someplace and we had to spend the night in the hall?" she whispered. "I'd kill myself, I just know I would!"

Maybe I'd kill myself because she had found that damned key, I thought bleakly, as I followed her inside. The only reason I was there was to make sure she hadn't been lying when I made the pitch about leaving a package with her that wonderful day just before Kluger had been arrested. A roll in the hay with Janice O'Brien had no place in my scheme of things, only I wasn't too sure just how I was going to break the news to her when the time came.

She found the switch and I stepped into the softly lit entrance hall, then had time for exactly one more step before the sky fell in. I vaguely heard the impact as something hard and unyielding slammed across the back of my head with brutal force. The pain exploded my eyeballs in a crackling fiery eruption that sent bolts of molten lightning sizzling into my brain, destroying it entirely in less than a split second, and I sank almost gratefully into a soft pile of cold dark ashes.

The pain inside my head made me wish I hadn't recovered consciousness quite so goddamned fast. Then I looked at my watch and realized, as near as I could figure it, I had been out cold for a minimum of twenty minutes. It felt like it took even longer to drag myself up from the floor onto my feet, but it didn't, of course.

I was still inside the softly lit entrance hall, only now the front door was shut tight behind me. I yelled, "Janice!" a couple of times and didn't get any answer, so I staggered into the living room, which was also softly lit. It looked like a playroom for maniacs, after a wet day had kept them inside too long. Every drawer had been pulled out of the bureau, and their contents scattered wildly across the floor. The cushions,

the upholstery of the couch and a couple of arm-
chairs, had all been slashed to ribbons so the stuffing
had spilled out everywhere. Even a couple of pictures
had been torn from the walls, then chopped into small
pieces.

The gun I'd taken from the bureau drawer on Diane
Kluger's advice bumped gently against my hip; I felt a
strong sense of relief once it was gripped tight in my
right hand. My foot slammed the bedroom door back
onto its hinges, then I saw that the havoc in there
was maybe even worse. The mattress had been
dragged from the bed onto the floor, then hacked
open so that the wool and cotton fiber stuffing had
spread across the floor, making it look like Christmas
in July.

Janice O'Brien lay on her back, spreadeagled across
the bedsprings, her bare feet dangling over the foot of
the bed. My feet dragged reluctantly when I moved
into the room and finally stopped beside the bed.
Slowly my mind absorbed the details, and for a moment some kind of neurotic logic made them seem like
a punishment for all the harsh things I had thought
about the girl while she was still alive.

There was the frozen terror in her wide-open eyes,
and a pitifully vulnerable look about her thin naked
body, still arched in mute protest against the unen-
durable pain inflicted upon it. Finally I forced myself
to look at the barbaric atrocities some sadist had inflicted on her narrow thighs with a heated knife-blade,
or something similar.

I fought down the rising nausea in my throat and
checked again. There was no blood, no bullet or knife
wound, so it figured to be the pain and shock that
had killed her. All the diamonds in the whole damned
world wouldn't be enough to justify what had been
done to Janice O'Brien, I thought dully, and felt the
cold hatred thrust its roots deep in the back of my
mind and start to grow. Hatred for the sadist responsible for the girl's death; and hatred for Mike Kluger,
because it could never have happened if he hadn't

involved the blonde in his conniving seven years back. Then also, with a vague sense of shock, I realized that Kluger's guilt was no greater than mine.

The palms of my hands were sweating profusely even before I heard the first police siren wailing in the distance.

chapter six

Panic cost me a couple of invaluable minutes while I just stood there, listening to that siren getting louder all the time. If they found me with Janice O'Brien's body, they would figure Kluger had left the diamonds with her for safekeeping until he got out of jail. Then, when she didn't hand them over, he'd tortured her to find out the truth that maybe she'd cashed in on the loot while he was still in the pen.

It would be an open-and-shut case that would send me to the gas chamber; who the hell would ever believe my wild story about being a guy named Farrel, who just happened to be impersonating Kluger at the time? Even if they did, I realized hopelessly, it wouldn't make any real difference because I'd still have the same motivation for torturing the girl that Kluger had, anyway.

The sound of the siren rose to a crescendo, then started to die away as the police car came to a stop outside the apartment house. My legs started working again and took me back through the living room into the entrance hall. I switched off the light, then eased the front door open an inch at a time. Everything was quiet outside, so I stepped out of the apartment and closed the front door behind me before I started for the stairs.

Just before I reached the stairway, I heard the street door slam open, then heavy footsteps pounded up the first flight. If I kept on going I was about to meet the cops on their way up. I turned back. A thin shaft of light suddenly spilled from under the door of the apartment next to the one containing Janice O'Brien's body. I figured the noise of the siren must have wakened the occupant, and almost simultaneously I hammered on the door with the butt of the gun still held in my hand.

"Who's that?" a feminine voice called from inside.

"Police!" I growled. "Open up."

There were a frantic few seconds while I just stood waiting, listening to those heavy feet pounding closer toward the third floor. Then I heard the snick as the chain was withdrawn a moment before the door opened. The flat of my hand helped it open wide enough to let me in, then I slammed the door shut again and replaced the night chain.

"What's going on?" a bewildered voice demanded.

I turned around slowly and leaned against the door while the voice's owner watched me in wide-eyed bewilderment. A tousled raven's wing of rich jet-black hair tumbled down across her forehead and across one eye, giving her an attractively wanton appearance. The sharp planes of her face showed a quick intelligence, and the broad mouth a sense of humor, I noted hopefully, even if her dark eyes were replacing their look of bewilderment with one of deep suspicion. She wore a bikini pajama outfit of white nylon; a halter top did nothing to conceal the ripe perfection of her high breasts, and the pocket-handkerchief briefs merely emphasized the proud curves of her hips. If I'd had the time to think about sex right then, I couldn't have picked a better moment.

"You're no police officer," she said accusingly.

"Look," I said desperately, "you've got to believe me! The girl in the next apartment is dead, but I had nothing to do with it. If the police find me, I'll never convince them that it's the truth!"

"If you didn't kill her, then who did?" she asked in a low voice.

"I don't know," I told her. "Whoever it was must have been hidden inside the apartment when we walked in, and slugged me on the back of the head.

When I woke up they'd gone, and I found the girl's body in the bedroom."

She nuzzled her lower lip between her teeth for a few seconds while she looked at me thoughtfully. "There's one thing I can check," she murmured. "You should have a bump on the back of your head, at least."

I moved closer to her until our bodies were almost touching, and it didn't seem to worry her at all. She put her arm around my neck, and I winced as her fingers probed callously until she was satisfied.

"That part of it's true." She let her arm drop back to her side. "There's a lump okay, and the skin's broken in a couple of places." She looked at the red smear on her fingertips and wrinkled her nose distastefully.

The heavy feet thudded past outside the door, then the door buzzer of the next apartment sounded on a low, continuous note.

"I could believe the rest of it maybe, if you didn't have that gun in your hand," the brunette said slowly.

A heavy thud came a moment after the buzzer had stopped, then we heard the heavy feet moving through the next apartment with ominous speed. I took a deep breath, then slid the gun back into my hip pocket.

"That's better." The girl's voice was completely calm, and I was dimly grateful she hadn't dissolved into screaming hysterics the moment I busted in on her.

"They'll search the whole building once they've found the body," I whispered. "This will be about the first place they'll look."

"What do you want me to do?"

"Hide me someplace until they've gone."

"I must be out of my mind!" She shook her head slowly. "All right. Get into the bedroom, take off your clothes and get into bed—quickly!"

"Hunh?" I gaped at her.

"Don't argue!" she said savagely. "You don't have the time."

She was so obviously right, I was halfway toward the bedroom before she'd finished speaking. Once inside, I stripped off my clothes in a series of frenzied movements, like the leader of some nudist colony caught with his clothes on when company's coming. When I got down to my shorts, I dived into the bed and pulled the covers up over my shoulders.

The brunette came in a couple of seconds later on her way to the bathroom, holding her smeared fingertips out in front of her like they were unclean. She was still in there when the doorbell sounded, sending my nerve ends gibbering around in small circles. After a little while, they got tired of just pressing the doorbell, and started pounding on the door. The girl reappeared with spotless fingertips and walked unhurriedly back into the living room, like she was stone-deaf or something.

"Who is it?" she called out.

"Police, lady," a gruff voice bellowed from outside. "Open up."

"Be a minute," she yelled, then came back into the bedroom.

I watched her take a silk robe out of the closet and put it on carefully, like she wanted to make sure she looked her best for the flatfoot outside.

"Hurry it up, huh?" I pleaded.

"He just woke me up with all that noise, remember?" she said coolly. "If I answer the door too quickly, he'll start wondering why I was up at this hour in the morning."

"You're right," I admitted.

She gave me a parting shot on her way out. "You always sleep with your hair brushed so neatly?"

I rumpled my hair savagely after she'd gone, then turned my head away from the bedroom door and listened. Muffled voices murmured for a while, then steadily grew louder as they came closer. I closed my eyes, half-buried my head in the cushion, and started a gentle, rhythmic snore.

"No, Officer," the brunette's voice said evenly, "we

didn't hear a thing until you knocked on our door. "She laughed softly. "My husband's *still* asleep!"

"Yeah." The harsh voice sounded startlingly close. "I can see that." A tinge of envy crept into the voice. "Chee! I wish I knew the secret of sleeping like that!"

"It's no trick," the girl said wearily. "All you have to do is get loaded every night."

"Like that, huh?" The cop sounded sympathetic. "I'm sorry, lady."

"Don't be," she said tartly. "You should see him sober!"

Their voices receded again, and after a couple more minutes I heard the front door close. The brunette reappeared in the doorway and smiled at me.

"He's gone," she said. "You can get dressed again now. I'll make some coffee."

By the time I'd gotten dressed again, she had the coffee ready in the living room. I sat down in an armchair facing her, the coffee table between us, and lit a cigarette.

"I can't tell you how grateful I am," I said awkwardly. "If you hadn't believed me, I'd be on my way to the gas chamber by now!"

"Forget it," she said easily, and handed me a cup of coffee. "What are you going to do now?"

"They'll have the building covered until morning, anyway," I said. "I'm sorry, but that means I have to stay here until then."

"You can sleep on the couch." Her voice was indifferent. "I'm Maggie Smith, by the way. It's a lousy name but nobody ever has any trouble pronouncing it right!"

I grinned for the first time since I'd been inside her apartment. "It sounds real great to me," I said. "It should be spelled out in neon lights across the sky, 'My benefactor, Maggie Smith, with all sincere good wishes—Mike!'"

"That's enough of that, Mike," she sniffed. "And call me Maggie. I've got no secrets hidden from you after the way I was dressed when you burst in here."

"It's going to haunt me the rest of my life," I groaned. "I just didn't have the time to fully appreciate it right then."

"Too bad!" she said tightly. "That was the only chance you'll ever have, I can promise you."

"Don't make any promises you can't guarantee somebody else won't break for you, Maggie," I said nastily, "like me, for instance."

"That sounds like my cue to retire for the rest of the night, having first locked the bedroom door on the inside," she said icily.

"I was only kidding," I gulped. "Stay and talk for a while, huh? I can use the company."

"All right," she said ungraciously, "but just for a few minutes. What do you want to talk about?"

I looked around desperately, then said, "It's a real nice apartment. Been here long, Maggie?"

"A couple of weeks." She sounded bored. "It's only a temporary arrangement."

Right then I heard it again—that warning bell in the back of my mind that had been making faint noises right from the time I first set foot inside the door—only up until now I'd been too damned preoccupied to listen. I put the coffee cup back onto the table carefully, and watched her face.

"Two weeks?" I said casually. "Now there's a co-incidence! It's about the same time the girl who was killed tonight had been in her apartment."

"Really?" Her voice was nonchalant, but a sudden alertness gleamed in her dark eyes.

"The more I think about it, Maggie, the more I think you're a girl in a million," I went on in the same casual tone. "Any normal dame would have flipped when I busted in on her in the middle of the night with a gun in my hand—and double-flipped when I told her there was a corpse in the next-door apartment, but I wasn't responsible. But you? Right off you checked on the one point of my story that could be checked—the bump on the back of my head. Then the way you instantly figured out the perfect gimmick to hide me from the cops by passing me off as your husband—the lush!—was terrific!"

"Please!" She yawned gently. "One vote of thanks is quite enough, Mike!"

"Mike what?" I asked softly.

"What do you mean?"

"You told me your name was Maggie Smith; I told you in a roundabout kind of way that mine was Mike, and you never even bothered to ask what was my last name."

"Maybe I wasn't interested," she snapped.

"Maybe you knew it already?" I snarled. "Maybe you knew Mike Kluger's old flame was in town, and she could be the one who'd kept those uncut diamonds safely for him until he got out of jail? So maybe you moved into this apartment to keep a permanent stake-out on Janice for when I got back into town?"

Her broad mouth curved into a mocking smile. "Why would I want to do that, Mike?"

"If you were a policewoman you'd have arrested me the moment I put the gun away," I said, "and you're just not the type to be working with creeps like Edwards, or Lou Stern. Besides, they wouldn't think this way, in terms of stake-outs and such; violence is the only kind of action they understand." I paused for a moment, then the obvious answer hit me right between the eyes.

"Maggie, honey," I said happily. "Just how long have you been in the insurance business?"

She scowled at me murderously. "Oh, you're so damned smart all of a sudden, aren't you, Kluger! Sure, I work for Global, what else? And Janice O'Brien was my assignment—"

"While Mike Kluger was Halloran's assignment?" I interrupted her.

"We work as a team," she snapped, "and—" She stopped suddenly, her eyes furious at her own stupidity.

"A team," I repeated softly. "Partners? And when one partner has Mike Kluger holed up in her apartment, hiding from the cops because they figure he murdered his girl friend, the least she can do is keep the other partner informed about it." I smiled thinly at her. "The coffee! Of course! You've got a phone in the kitchen, right?"

The sudden increased fury in her eyes was the only answer I needed. "Halloran won't have any problem explaining to the fuzz why he's calling at this hour in the morning," I thought out loud. "His insurance identification is good enough. I guess you're working with Lieutenant Cromby in this, even if you're not working real close to him? So we'll hear the doorbell any time now, right?"

"Don't ask me!" Maggie said icily. "All this is your own idea."

I took the gun out of my hip pocket and held it so the barrel pointed vaguely in her direction.

"You hear this good!" I grated. "If the cops pick me up here, it means I'm facing one murder rap I can't beat. So I won't let it happen, even if I have to kill to stop it happening. You got that, Maggie?"

For the first time a look of genuine alarm showed on her face. "I—understand!" she said weakly.

"So you do exactly like I tell you," I said harshly, "or you're dead! When the doorbell goes, you answer it, and tell Halloran everything's okay, I'm fast asleep in the bedroom. I'll be behind the door when you open it, and if anything goes wrong, I'll let you have it first!"

"I'll do exactly what you say, Mike." She gulped nervously. "I promise!"

"You can start right now," I growled, "by taking off that robe."

A look of horror spread rapidly across her face. "You wouldn't—you couldn't?" She shivered suddenly. "Mike, please! I'm just not the kind of girl who—I'll do anything you say, I told you that, I promised! I meant every word of it, Mike, and—"

"Ah, shut up, and get out of that robe!" I snarled at her. "I want a real good distraction to keep Halloran's eyes from wandering too much when he walks in, that's all. What kind of a creep do you think I am, anyway?"

"Oh, Mike!" She shuddered in grateful relief. "I'm sorry, I thought you meant——"

"Yeah!" I nodded impatiently. "I know what you thought I meant. So now, will you get out of that robe?"

She stood up obediently and took off the robe, then smiled at me uncertainly. "You know something funny?" she said in a small voice. "The first time I saw you like this, it didn't bother me at all—but now it does!"

"You know something?" I grinned bleakly at her. "I was about to say the same thing."

Her face suddenly crimsoned and she turned away from me abruptly, still leaving me with nothing to complain about—the rear view was just as enticing.

"It's a lousy trick, so I'll try and stop leering," I told her. "But you'd better lose your inhibitions before Halloran gets here, or he'll know there's something wrong."

"I'll be all right," she said tersely, and turned toward me again. "You want some more coffee?"

"No, that was just fine," I said. "Is your relationship with Halloran strictly business?"

"But strictly!" she snapped. "He's a clever insurance investigator, but as a person he makes my spine crawl."

"I get the same feeling," I agreed. "I wouldn't trust him to see his own mother safely across the street, if he had her insured for ten bucks!"

"Well, it's nice to hear the opinion of a man with such integrity as Mike Kluger!" she sneered. "You'll pardon me, if——"

Then the doorbell rang, and she nearly jumped out of her halter top, which wouldn't have been much of a trick, at that.

I moved fast across the room and stood with my back to the wall so I'd be hidden behind the door when she opened it. Then I gestured with the gun. Maggie

Smith fixed a bright smile on her face, then walked across the room with a wonderful, free-swinging bounce and opened the door.

"It's all right," she said quickly in a whispering voice. "He's fast asleep in the bedroom. Just don't make too much noise!"

"Sure," Halloran's irritating nasal drawl answered. "That's fine, now we can—" His voice thickened suddenly. "Hey! Kluger must be sick, going to sleep while you're waltzing around in a sexy outfit like that!"

Maggie moved back into my range of vision, with a sickly smile on her face. "What with all the excitement, I forgot I was still in my pajamas," she said weakly.

"And I'm real glad you forgot, honey!" I never heard a voice leer, but Halloran's did right then. "You've got a lot of good points I never even knew about before—"

Then he came into my line of vision, a brown fedora pushed back on his head and a shabby raincoat hanging from his shoulders. Before Maggie had a chance to anticipate him, he reached out and squeezed her breasts hard with both hands. A look of revulsion showed on her face, then she glanced over his shoulder and saw me poised in back of him, the gun butt raised ready.

"You could take off your hat first!" she snapped at him.

"Sorry!" he chuckled dirtily, then took off his hat. A split second later the gun butt bounced off the back of his head, and he slumped sideways onto the floor.

"Thanks, Maggie," I said in genuine appreciation. "The timing was beautiful."

"If I was sure you could keep a secret, I'd tell you that last bit was a pleasure." She scowled down at Halloran's inert body on the floor and made a contemptuous sound deep in her throat. "What happens now?"

"When Halloran wakes up, tell him how I forced you to open the door and play dumb because I was right in back of it with a gun in my hand," I said. "For what it's worth, you can tell him I didn't torture Janice O'Brien to death, but I'm going to find out who did, and soon."

"I'll tell him," she said doubtfully, "but I don't think he'll buy that part about the O'Brien girl."

"Then—and this goes for both of you—if you tell the cops what happened tonight," I snarled, "it will mean you've destroyed your last hope of getting those diamonds back!"

Maggie Smith massaged her lower lip between her teeth for a few moments, then nodded reluctantly. "I hate to admit it, but you make sense, Kluger."

I stripped the raincoat from Halloran awkwardly, then put it on myself. The brunette watched with open curiosity while I pushed the fedora onto the back of my head.

"What is it?" she asked finally. "Fancy dress night?"

"It's just that I always wanted to look like an insurance investigator," I explained seriously. "Got any claims you want investigated?"

She still had a blank expression on her face when I walked out of the apartment.

At this time in the small hours I figured the lighting would be real dim in the lobby, and it was. The uniformed cop who slouched comfortably in a chair—strategically placed so he could watch the door without being seen immediately by anyone coming into the building—nodded as I went past. There was no point in him taking any further interest because he knew who I was—the insurance investigator in a dirty raincoat and fedora he'd checked into the place about fifteen minutes before. What goes in, has to come out; and he had no reason to suspect there was anything different wrapped up in the same package that was going out right then.

An early dawn was streaking the sky as I walked down the street, and it looked like it was going to be a fine day. I hoped it would be, because I could use a fine day.

chapter seven

I let myself into the house with the door key, and closed the door very gently so it only made a faint click as it shut. Halfway across the front hall I suddenly froze when a drowsy voice called from the living room.

"Mike? Is that you?"

Diane sat up and yawned, then swung her legs off the couch in an easy movement. "I thought I'd wait up for you." She yawned again, then stretched her arms over her head luxuriously. "What time is it?"

"A little after six."

"You have had a long night of it, Mike Farrel!" Her voice sounded amused, but there was something quite different underneath. "My husband's girl friend must have been really stunning."

"She was a singer in a club owned by Chris Edwards, and she wasn't much, poor kid," I said wearily. "Now she's nothing."

"What do you mean?"

"She's dead." I slumped into the nearest armchair and lay my head back against the cushioned padding. "Somebody tortured her to death."

"Mike!"

I told her the details, from when I met Janice in Hagan's Bar, until the time I left Maggie Smith's apartment and came back to the house. Diane listened intently, her corn-colored hair pleasantly mussed and the rosy flush of sleep still showing on her plump cheeks. Her wide, generous mouth tightened into a straight line as she heard what happened to the blonde singer.

"Even if Halloran and the Smith girl don't tell the police you were there," she said in a low voice after I'd finished, "will it make any difference? I mean, won't Lieutenant Cromby still be convinced that you killed her?"

"Maybe," I said. "For sure he'll be around asking questions any time now."

"I can tell him you spent the night here—with me?"

"He won't have any trouble proving I left Edwards' place with the girl," I said slowly, "and he's sure to find the hack driver who took us from the club to the apartment house. That would be around three A.M. when we got there, I guess. It's the next three hours up until I got back here that worry me. If you said I got home sometime between four and four-thirty, it would help a lot, Diane."

"It's no trouble," she said evenly."

"Only how would you know I got home at that time in the morning?" I groaned. "You'd be fast asleep when I got in!"

"Not if you'd forgotten to take a door key," she murmured.

"You are nothing, if not a genius," I told her admiringly.

"My genius tells me more," she smiled broadly. "You'd better get into bed fast, Mike Farrel, before that lieutenant gets here and finds you fully dressed, with the bed in your room obviously unslept in."

"I don't know what I'd do without you, Diane," I admitted.

"Put that door key, and the gun, back in the bureau drawer on your way through the hall," she added. "The door key is the one you forgot to take with you, and I'm the one who holds the license for the gun, remember?"

"I'm crushed!" I whimpered, and dragged myself out of the chair, then started toward the door.

"Your room is the second door on your left, around

the corner in the hall. I put your things in there after you left tonight," Diane said in a studiously neutral voice. "So you'll know you're in the right room when you see them."

"Thank you!" I said, with immense dignity.

She giggled suddenly. "Tell me something, Mike Farrel. How did you plan on finding your room? With a divining rod?"

There had to be a logical answer to that, only I I couldn't think of it right then so I just kept on going. I followed her instructions, found the right room, and was in bed a couple of minutes later.

I woke out of a drugged sleep reluctantly, convinced it couldn't have been more than a minute since I'd closed my eyes, and found Diane leaning over me, shaking my shoulder vigorously.

"All right, already!" I glared at her balefully. "So where's the fire?"

"In the living room, and its name is Cromby!" She straightened up gracefully. "He's being very polite, but underneath he's seething, I can tell."

She looked fresh as paint, wearing a dusty-pink dacron blouse and peacock blue stretch slacks.

"What time did you get up?" I asked.

"I stayed up after you went to bed," she said. "I'd had a night's sleep on the couch before you got home. You'd better hurry, Mike Farrel. I don't think it would be wise to keep the lieutenant waiting."

"Okay, tell him I'll be right there," I grunted. "What time is it now?"

"Around ten-thirty." She turned away from me, paused for a moment while her hand surreptitiously felt for the edge of the bedside table, then once she'd found it and reorientated herself, she walked confidently toward the door.

"How do you know what time it is, Diane, when you can't look at a watch?" I asked curiously.

She stopped in the doorway for a moment, and her shoulders made a quivering movement. For a moment I figured that the question had upset her and she felt embarrassed, then heard the gurgling laughter in her voice when she spoke.

"It's this brand new gimmick they've got now," she spluttered. "What do they call it—radio?"

After she'd left the room, I had a quick shower and shave, got dressed, and was on my way out in not more than ten minutes. When I came into the living room, Lieutenant Cromby was pacing up and down in front of the couch like a long distance runner who's run out of space but still needs the exercise.

"You sure take your own time, Kluger!" he snarled, by way of a greeting.

"Ten minutes back I was still fast asleep," I said in a wounded voice. "What did you expect? Instant dressing?"

His hard eyes bored into me for a long moment. "Where did you go after you left the bar last night?" he rasped.

"The Blue Goose," I said.

"After that?"

"I took Janice O'Brien home to her apartment."

"About what time was that?"

I thought about it, without hurrying, "Around three this morning, I guess."

"What time was it when you left her apartment?" he asked in a suddenly gentle voice.

"I never left it."

"You what?"

"I never left it because I never went there in the first place," I said innocently. "I said good night to Janice in the lobby."

"You're lying, Kluger," he snapped. "I had a tail on you the whole time, and he says you went into the building with the girl around three A.M. okay, but he never saw you come out again!"

Cromby was a good cop, I figured. Even when he was lying in the course of duty he didn't like it, and it showed in his voice.

"Have it your way, Lieutenant." I shrugged easily. "So I'm still inside that building, right?"

"Your wife says you got home sometime between four and four-thirty," he kept right on pitching. "If you left that girl in the lobby, how come it took you a whole hour to get back here?"

"I walked," I said, and let a bored note creep into my voice. "You got a law against that, Lieutenant? It had been a hell of a long day, with people like you and that insurance investigator pushing me all the time. When a guy gets home after seven years, and finds both his wife, and an old girl friend waiting for him, it makes for a king-sized emotional problem. Last night, at the club, I told Janice to forget it. That's why I walked home from her apartment house. I needed the time to get adjusted a little. Everything had been going too fast from the moment I got off the bus."

I lit a cigarette, then looked at him with a sudden impatience. "Just what the hell is this all about, Lieutenant? You got a reason for a million questions, or is it just go-worry-Kluger-time again?"

"Janice O'Brien was murdered last night," he said quietly, "or around three-thirty this morning, to be accurate!"

"Murdered?" I stared at him blankly for a few moments, then turned away. "How did it happen?"

"She was tortured by some sadist who gets his kicks by burning a woman's flesh," he said in an ugly voice. "Somewhere along the line, her heart quit. The doctor figures she had a congential weakness there from the time she was born, and probably never even knew it."

"Who would do a thing like that?" I muttered.

"Ask the person who called in and told us Mike Kluger was murdering his girl friend and we should get out there fast and stop it," he said flatly.

I swung around toward him again. "And you think I did?"

"You don't have any alibi."

"I told you what time I left her in the lobby. My wife told you what time I got home."

"What kind of an alibi is that?" He shrugged.

"You said she was tortured—burned?"

"That's right." He hesitated a fraction of a second, then added, "The whole apartment had been ripped apart, too."

"So somebody ripped up the apartment looking for something they didn't find? Then they tortured Janice to make her tell them where to find it?" I said. "Is that how you figure it?"

"I guess so."

"The only thing poor Janice could've had of any real value would be those uncut diamonds, supposing I'd left them with her before I was arrested." I shook my head despairingly. "I'm Mike Kluger, remember? —the guy who heisted those rocks in the first place. Wouldn't I *know* what I did with the goddamned things? Would I need to go looking for them in Janice's place? Need to torture her into telling me if I'd left them with her?"

"No, to all of those things," he said brusquely. "That's why I wasn't here about three hours back to book you on a homicide rap, Kluger."

"The hell with you!" I snarled. "So why make me dance through the hoops, if you knew it wasn't me all the time?"

"I just don't think it was you," he answered coldly. "I don't know it wasn't you. It's possible she double-crossed you while you were in the pen, and you tried to torture the truth out of her about what she'd done with your loot. But for the time being, I don't believe that. So it has to be somebody else. You got any ideas?"

"No," I whispered, "but I'm going to find out."

"I wouldn't," he said. "You're in enough trouble already."

Diane appeared in the doorway with a polite smile on her face. "Some coffee, Lieutenant?"

"No, thanks, Mrs. Kluger." His voice was suddenly gentle and pleasant. "I'm just about to leave."

"I'll have your breakfast ready in the kitchen, Mike, after you've seen the lieutenant to the door," she said.

"Thanks, honey," I told her.

She went back to the kitchen, and I walked with Cromby to the front door.

"I won't say it's been a pleasure, Lieutenant." I held the door open for him. "Or invite you to drop in any time, because I know you will."

He made no attempt to walk outside, so that left me holding the door wide open like I was expecting somebody else to walk in.

"You know what seven years in the pen can do for a man?" he said idly, like he was doodling with words instead of a pencil. "Both physically and mentally, I mean?"

"I guess it won't make any difference if I do or don't," I said wearily. "I have the feeling you're about to tell me, anyway."

"Physically, it makes a lot of men get fat and flabby, lose their hair, sometimes their teeth," he said. "Alters their voices very often, too. When a guy picks up the habit of always whispering and talking out of the side of his mouth for a number of years, sometimes it's hard to break. Then, if a guy serves something better than five years, it often makes his brain a little flabby, too."

"It's an education just listening to you, Lieutenant!" I said. "Don't tell me you do card tricks, too?"

"I was about to do something I wouldn't have believed possible thirty minutes back," he said dryly, "and that's pay you a compliment, Kluger. San Quentin must have been good for you, because you came out a better man than you were when you went in!"

"Am I hearing you right?" I gurgled.

"Sure, you hear me good," he said, nodding emphatically. "You're in fine physical shape, you haven't lost any hair or teeth. Your voice has deepened, and your vocabulary's improved out of sight! And you're thinking a hell of a lot faster—and smarter—than you did around the time I picked you up in New York."

"I would bust right out crying in pure gratitude," I told him, "only I figure you have an angle someplace in all this crud. My breakfast's getting cold, so do me a favor and come right out with it?"

"No angles, Kluger, it's the truth!" He walked past me onto the front porch, then paused a moment and stared hard at my face.

"You know something?" A slow grin of something close to triumph spread across his thick-set face. "Now —for the first time since you got back, Kluger—you look worried."

I watched until I saw him get into his car at the curb. Then I closed the door and walked back to the kitchen. Diane was sitting down with a cup of coffee, looking very comfortable and relaxed; I felt a stab of envy as I wondered just how good it must be to feel that way.

"Help yourself, Mike Farrel." She waved her hand toward the stove. "What isn't in the pan keeping hot, is cold and on the table."

"Thanks," I told her and helped myself.

"I take it the lieutenant has gone?" she said as I sat down opposite her, with a stacked plate of hotcakes and bacon.

"Gone, and left me worried," I growled.

"He thinks you killed the girl?"

"No. He thinks seven years in San Quentin was the best thing that ever happened to Mike Kluger. Something like a college education, only better!"

I interspersed the hotcakes with a detailed account of our conversation and that final virtuoso performance Cromby pulled at the front door.

"Maybe he was just trying to bait Mike Kluger in a new kind of way?" Diane said, but the doubtful sound in her voice said she didn't believe it either.

"That's stupid, and you know it, and Cromby isn't," I said gloomily. "The more I see of that guy, the more respect I have for him. He's a cop in the best sense of the word."

"He's about the finest man I've ever met, I think," Diane said softly. "His wife died suddenly about three years back, and I think he must have loved her very much. Underneath that hard-boiled front, I think he's a very kind man—and a very lonely one, too."

"Well!" I gaped at her. "Since when has there been all this hearts and flowers routine between you and the lieutenant?"

She laughed easily. "I guess it did sound like that, didn't it? I told you all kinds of people took a sudden interest in me when they heard my husband would be coming home in a couple of weeks. The lieutenant was one of them, of course. He visited two or three times before you arrived. He was always very official, and kept warning me about all the unpleasant things that would happen to my husband if he didn't hand over the diamonds to the police.

"But the last time, he relaxed a little for five whole minutes, and asked about my blindness. I told him about the next operation coming up, and he mentioned his wife had trouble with her eyesight a few months before she died—that was all."

"Uh-huh," I said vaguely. "So let's concentrate on Cromby, the cop, and skip Cromby, the loneliest of them all in the bleeding hearts club, why don't we?"

Her face stiffened as if I'd suddenly slapped her. "Whatever you think best, Mike Farrel," she said icily.

"Cromby the cop deals in facts—keeps them in a cross-indexed file, for quick reference," I went on. "Every new fact gets filed, and if one comes along that just doesn't jibe with his previous references, he takes it right out of the file and has a good close look at it."

"Now say it again, but differently, so I can understand?" she requested.

"Okay. He was the guy who went all the way to New York to arrest your husband in the first place," I said. "Maybe he got to know the real Mike Kluger fairly well during the trip back, the trial, and everything. The next time he meets him is seven years later, his first day of freedom from San Quentin. Like Cromby said, a long stretch in prison can do a lot of things to a man, one way and another, but this is the first time he's ever seen it not only improve a guy's physical health, but make him twice as smart mentally at the same time!"

"Even if you're right," she argued, "what does it prove? That he's found a new fact for that cross-indexed file you mentioned before. Nothing more, Mike Farrel."

"Not yet," I said moodily. "But he won't let it alone. He saw it worried me, so now it's going to worry him until he finds out why. And sometime he's going to come up with a real fantastic idea he'll laugh at the first time out—a real wild theory to fit his conflicting facts: Why is Mike Kluger changed so much for the better after all that time in the pen? Answer: Because this isn't the same Mike Kluger Cromby arrested in New York; this is a smart phony trading on his strong physical resemblance to Kluger, to impersonate him long enough to grab the loot and disappear before anyone else gets wise. You know something, Diane? When he takes a second look at that wild idea, Cromby won't laugh at all."

"You could be right," she said. "But what can you do about it?"

"All I can do is move a hell of a lot faster than I have up until now," I grunted.

"To find the diamonds, you mean?"

"The diamonds—and whoever killed Janice O'-Brien," I said.

"Isn't that the lieutenant's responsibility?" she asked softly.

"Sure, it is," I said. "But it's only his badge that gives it to him. Guilt is something that gives you bigger responsibility—or you can put that the other way around if you want, and it still comes out the same. Three people are responsible for Janice O'Brien's death: whoever it was that actually killed her is one; the second is your husband by placing her in a potentially dangerous situation just before he was arrested; and I'm the third, because while I was pretending to be your husband last night, I placed her dead-center in a real dangerous situation that resulted in her death!"

"You can't blame yourself for the girl's death, Mike Farrel," Diane said in a warm, sympathetic voice. "That would be stupid."

"I took Mike Kluger's name, and by a strong physical resemblance, I took his body in a way," I told her. "Then I took his place in the scheme of things for a while. But I found out last night that you can't stop right there, because your actions are based on his actions—and however far back he made them, makes no difference at all. It was the real Mike Kluger who first started Janice O'Brien toward the terrible death that came to her last night, but it was me playing Mike Kluger earlier last night that altered her death from a probability to a certainty.

"I can't ever go back to being Mike Farrel, just by telling myself what happened was all Kluger's fault, don't you see that? How do I know what the real Mike Kluger would have done, if he'd been here to answer the phone when she called? That's why I have to even the score for Janice O'Brien by finding her killer, because then Mike Kluger will have atoned for his guilt—and I can be Mike Farrel again, with no nightmares to haunt me for the rest of my life!"

Diane took a deep breath, then exhaled slowly. "I still think you're wrong, but there's no point in arguing about it now. I think we have to be very practical, and decide what you're going to do next, Mike Farrel."

"Okay," I said. "The first thing I'm going to do is find out more about Mike Kluger."

"Why?"

"I've got a strong hunch that if I can get to know enough about him, it will be the quickest way to find the diamonds, and Janice's killer."

"How are you going to find out more about my husband?"

"You're going to tell me, Diane," I said decisively.

"It's nice of you to let me know!" Her voice was

genuinely amused. "I imagine you don't want total recall, so you'll ask some questions?"

"I want to play the lieutenant's cross-indexed game," I said seriously. "Put a couple of different-sounding facts together, and hope you can come up with a third, or fourth even, that will make the first two jell."

"I hope I can, too," she said. "Shoot!"

"You said he tricked you into marriage in the first place, and then it was no kind of marriage in the six weeks you had together before he went to New York?"

"That's right."

"Janice O'Brien said last night she never did understand why I—meaning the real Kluger of course—had ever married you. 'First you were crazy about the other one,' she said, 'then you got so mad when she dumped you and went off with that other guy, you turned around and married her sister before you knew what you were doing, even.' That's how Janice said it. How would you say it, Diane?"

A look of bitter understanding showed briefly on her face, then she nodded dully. "I think I'd say it about the same way she said it."

"Tell me about your sister?" I suggested.

"Deirdre?" She lifted her head unconsciously, as if the mere sound of the name would bring some new treachery to be guarded against. "My kid sister." Her mouth twisted ironically. "By the time she was seventeen and I was nineteen, she was already ten years older than I in everything but years. Father had died when we were both very young; Mother worked hard to support us and I guess it didn't leave her much time to worry about what we did when she wasn't around.

"Anyway, Deirdre started going steady with this Mike Kluger, and I got to meet him a couple of times. He made me flip the first time I ever saw him—those dark good looks, his immense sophistication, and a kind of animal magnetism. Then they were formally engaged, going to be married, and I figured that was the end of it for me. Mother got sick again and it was real bad this time, and I spent nearly all my time looking after her.

"Then Deirdre just didn't come home at all one night. I didn't dare tell Mother because of what it might do to her, so I worried frantically until we got a letter two days later saying she'd met the most wonderful man—you know the kind of mush!—and had gone with him to New York and they were going to be married there. A postscript said she'd write to Mike Kluger in the next couple of days, and maybe it would be better if we let him hear it from her first.

"My mother was dying, but I didn't know it then. All I knew was she got worse each day, and the doctor said she had to have complete rest and absolute quiet if I wanted her to have any chance at all. The third night after we'd received Deirdre's letter, Mike Kluger visited. He was like a maniac—he'd just gotten her Dear John letter an hour before—and he pushed me back from the door into the living room, raving at the top of his voice that she couldn't do this to him.

"I tried to tell him to keep quiet because of Mother being sick but he didn't even listen. Finally I dragged him into my room and closed the door, thinking I could eventually talk sense into him, and meanwhile Mother wouldn't be worried by the noise."

Diane laughed suddenly. "My God! I never realized before just how corny this sounds when you say it out loud. It's strictly an old-time melodrama!"

"And you made one of the virgin's classic mistakes by thinking your room would be just the place to talk sense?" I added helpfully.

"He blamed the whole family for it," Diane continued, and now her voice had an undercurrent of laughter bubbling through it, "so if he couldn't have Deirdre, the family would have to compensate him for his loss."

"And that meant you?" I said.

"That was when the real melodrama started. I had the classic choice straight out of a Greek tragedy—either I let him rob me of my most precious jewel, or

I could scream for help and most likely kill my mother at the same time!"

Her voice sobered abruptly. "The full irony of it all was that I still felt the same way about him as I had from the first time we met. The great drama played out in my room that night was really all my daydreams come true. When it was all over and he started mumbling he was sorry, I told him I wasn't, and how I'd always loved him madly—and so on. I guess it did so much for his ego he flipped completely. He said it proved that Deirdre was the wrong girl for him in the first place, so would I marry him?

"So we got married three weeks later, and I think he'd cooled off even before then, but he didn't have the courage to stop the marriage. You know the rest; after a lousy six weeks he just disappeared, and the next thing I knew was when I read about his arrest in New York. My mother died two days after the verdict, and that was the end of it."

"Only he came back here secretly for twenty-four hours, just a few days before his arrest, and spent the whole time with Janice O'Brien," I said slowly. "The way she told it, it was the most wonderful day of her whole life. They went to the beach in the morning, the amusement park in the afternoon—"

"Mike Kluger always was very big in amusement parks," she said dryly. "I remember Deirdre croming home one night with a Kewpie doll under each arm that Mike had won for her displaying his prowess in a shooting gallery. He even did the same for me once. As I remember it cost him around twenty-five dollars to win me a doll that said *Mama!* about three times before the spring broke inside."

"The prize he won Janice cost him only twenty bucks, she said." I grinned for a moment. "Then they had an ecstatic night in a hotel: she delicately implied that was the time when she surrendered her most precious jewel—"

"I don't care to hear the intimate details especially," Diane said.

"I guess they're not important," I said with a shrug. "But Kluger—knowing Cromby was about to catch up with him any time within the next few days—still took the risk of coming back here where he was known and could easily be recognized. I don't believe he came back just for the pleasure of Janice's company. No woman would ever be that important to him. So he must have come back to stash his loot somewhere he was sure it would be safe until such time as he could pick it up again, right?"

"Of course!" Diane sounded impatient. "That's what the lieutenant thinks—what everybody thinks!"

"But I'm the only one who talked to Janice O'Brien last night," I snarled. "Two things! One: he was with her the whole time, morning, afternoon, and night! Two: he never gave her the jewels, a package, any damned thing at all to keep for him!"

"You're sure, Mike Farrel?" she said doubtfully.

"Sure, I'm sure!" I grated. "So where do we go from here?"

She shook her head. "I just don't know."

"Well," I said in a defiant voice that sounded childish even to my own ears, "I'm not going to sit around and wait for something to happen. I'm going right out and keep raising hell until something does happen!"

"Don't be so juvenile!" Diane said contemptuously, and that did it up just fine.

"And the hell with you, too!" I yelled at her. "There's a good chance—if I go out and wave your gun in enough faces—that maybe I'll get a couple of honest facts for a change!"

I stormed out of the kitchen through to the front hall, and stopped long enough to collect the gun and door key from the bureau drawer before I went out of the house. I could hear Diane's voice still calling my name frantically, the moment before I slammed the front door shut in back of me. Right then I didn't have the time to feel sorry for her. I was too busy feeling sorry for myself.

chapter eight

What I needed in this town more than anything else was an automobile, I realized bleakly, as I trudged along the sidewalk. It was five blocks to a busstop, and who knew when a bus would come along when you got there? A cruising cab in this neighborhood was about as usual a sight as a troop of can-can dancers high-kicking on the steps of the city hall.

I had walked about two blocks when a gray sedan pulled into the curb beside me, and an intelligent but anxious face, surmounted by a raven's wing of glossy black hair, looked out.

"Well," I sneered thinly, "if it isn't the ace insurance investigator herself!"

"Mike!" Maggie Smith's dark eyes pleaded with me. "Please get into the car. I have to talk with you, and it won't wait!"

She was the answer to a pedestrian's prayer, but I wasn't about to let her know it, so I played hard to get for a few seconds, then generously acceded to her request. She slammed the car out from the curb again, almost before I'd gotten the door shut, and went through the next intersection like it was Indianapolis.

"You never told me it was a suicide pact?" I yelled at her. "I'm too young to die, and anyway, the last way I want to go is like a pound of hamburger steak minced up in your lousy automobile!"

She took a quick glance in the rear-view mirror, then eased her foot off the gas pedal with obvious reluctance.

"I just wanted to make sure he wasn't following us," she said in a taut voice.

"Why don't you tell me the rules? I'd love to play!" I snarled. "Who's the *he* that's maybe following us?"

"Halloran," she said briefly.

"What happened to bust up your beautiful partnership, if you don't trust each other anymore?" I asked.

"You!" she snapped. "And I guess I didn't help any when I set him up last night for you to slug him, either! The one thing he'll never forgive is me telling him to take off his hat so it wouldn't get in the way of the gun butt you bounced off his head a couple of seconds later!"

"So Halloran's head, ego, and faith in his partner were hurt?" I shrugged. "So what?"

"Don't be so goddamned superior about this, Mike Kluger!" she said with an arctic bite in her voice. "The head about to topple into the basket could be yours."

"Well, that's different," I said uneasily. "Why didn't you say that before?"

"I've been trying to, ever since I stopped beside you at the curb," she said from between clenched teeth. "Now, will you listen?"

"Go right ahead," I told her.

"It's his vanity that's really hurt," she explained carefully. "He can understand that—with you behind the door with a gun held on me—I had no choice but to set him up like a prize duck. But that bit with the hat, and coming right after he'd pawed me—" She shook her head miserably. "That's what's burning him up right now. He's convinced we made a fool out of him, above and beyond what was necessary, and it was a big joke between us. I also suspect he thinks that bikini pajama outfit had been worn for your benefit, not his, and that we spent the time waiting for him in a kind of perpetual orgy!"

"You mean he's still sore at both of us?" I suggested.

"Sore enough to do something stupid if it will hurt us," she said soberly. "I told him what you said—if either of us told the police you were hiding in my apartment last night we'd lose our only chance of recovering the diamonds—and he seemed to accept the obvious logic in it. But now—"

"He's changed his mind?"

"I couldn't turn him out after you'd gone last night, not when he'd just been knocked unconscious," Maggie said. "So I let him sleep on the couch—and had to give him breakfast this morning. For a solid hour I just sat there, watching him get more vicious every minute. It started with the hat bit—he bet the two of us nearly died laughing while he lay unconscious on the floor. Then the orgy bit—he hadn't realized until he'd gotten a real good look at the way I was built, just how sexy a girl I was. With a dirty grin on his face, and that nasal voice whining at me the whole time! No wonder I'd pushed him away when he made a friendly pass—I must have been exhausted after the session I'd obviously had with Mike Kluger! He guessed a jaded nympho could get some kind of perverted kick out of lovemaking with a killer, his victim's blood still wet on his hands!"

"The lousy creep!" I said indignantly. "It was my blood that was still wet on your hands!"

"Then he started with the Sunday punch," she said bitterly. "What troubled him was, where did his duty lie, exactly? Just because his company wanted to recoup on an expensive claim—was this a good enough reason to let a killer go free, and a sex-confused girl ruin her life by not coming forward with vital evidence? He'd have to think it over, but the more he thought about it, the more he was convinced a killer couldn't go free just to save the company some money!"

"Those were his parting words?" I asked nervously.

"Almost," she said. "I told him I had to go out for a while—I just couldn't stand it anymore. When I was halfway out the door, he laughed nastily and said it wouldn't do any good tipping off my maniac-lover, because the police would grab him before he'd run a mile. So why didn't I rush straight over to Kluger's house and have one last passionate experience while I had the chance?"

"He's the kind of nut who would foul up everything just for his own stinking satisfaction!" I snarled. "But what the hell can I do about it?"

"There's one thing you can do which would cook his goose real crisp, Mike!" she said. "And I admit there's a lot of self-interest from my own point of view in this, but it's still your only chance!"

"So tell me?" I said sourly.

"If your turned the diamonds over to me right now," she said, "you'd get the reward from the company, and we could both go to the police and tell them what you've done. That would be the absolute proof you knew all the time where they were hidden, that you were the one person who had no need to search Janice O'Brien's apartment, and then torture her to death, to find out where they were hidden! You see?"

"I see," I grunted, "but I don't like it."

"Mike!" Her voice was crisp, and stung like a wet towel in the face. "Let's be honest. Like it or lump it, you don't have any choice about this. If Halloran says his piece before you've turned over the diamonds to me, it will be too late! We can run out of time at any moment."

"You're right!" I slumped back into the seat and made a few suggestions about Halloran's probable ancestry.

"I know." Maggie sighed in sympathy. "But it doesn't help. Where do we go to collect the diamonds?"

"You know where we can find Lou Stern?" I asked.

"Of course I do." Her eyes widened suddenly. "You mean, he's had them all the time?"

"He's part of it," I said smugly. "Stern first, then a couple of other places."

I could feel her almost twitching beside me with curiosity, but she managed to contain it through the rest of the drive although, by the agonized look on her face, it was taking years off her life.

Maybe fifteen minutes later she stopped the car outside an ancient warehouse that looked like it had hit its peak when the Sioux used it for storing scalps, then had steadily declined ever since.

"Mr. Stern's legitimate business, and cover for his other activities," Maggie announced. "But you know that already?"

"I'll be back in ten, fifteen minutes," I told her. "You wait for me."

"You're the boss, Mike!" She gave me a warm smile. "I'll wait."

There was a door marked OFFICE, and inside was a small room divided by a brass rail. The solitary chair on my side made it the reception area; the other half of the room was occupied by the work force, busy lacquering its nails.

"Where's Stern?" I asked.

The work force was an overweight blonde, her hair dyed to match the brass rail and teased into a gigantic ball of cotton candy. I peeked at her peekaboo nylon blouse and regretted it instantly; then the sight of her girdle so graphically outlined beneath her too-tight skirt did nothing to reassure me.

"Mr. Stern's in conference," she said, without bothering to look up from her nails.

"Who with? The Mafia?" I snarled.

I ducked under the brass rail and walked past her desk, toward the inner door.

"Hey!" she yelped, "You can't—" But by then it was too late because I already had.

Lou Stern looked up from behind a massive wooden desk as I came into the room, and a look of mild surprise showed on his cadaverous face. Sonny West had his back toward me, apparently absorbed in the view outside a grimy window.

"Mike?" Stern wheezed. "How come I didn't hear you announced?"

"Maybe you heard what happened to Janice O'Brien last night?" I snarled at him.

"A tough break," he said, and blinked slowly.

"I had an idea," I confided in a low, menacing voice. "I thought maybe Lou and Sonny suddenly got ambitious last night when they heard I was in the Blue Goose relighting an old flame with the singer there? It wouldn't have been very hard to get inside her apartment and wait for the two of us, would it? Then slug me and see what the girl's got to say with a little friendly persuasion?"

"I am shocked and horrified you could think such a dreadful thing about your friends, Mike," Lou wheezed. "It hits me right here!" He tapped his chest gently, then wheezed again.

"I got a hot flash for both of you," I said. "When I find the guy who did that to Janice, I'm going to kill him."

Sonny West finally turned around from the window and looked at me with an amused expression on his face.

"Since when did you get so tough, Mike?"

"Since Janice O'Brien died, maybe!" I smiled at him slowly, and put as much open contempt into the smile as I could. "You don't really think you scare anybody, Sonny?"

His eyes glittered suddenly, and the amused expression was abruptly wiped from his face. "Don't open your mouth so wide you split your skull, Kluger," he said in a flat voice.

"That's good advice." I nodded slowly, like I was impressed. "There's a chance I could be wrong—and if I am, I'm only insulting one of my future partners."

"Partners?" Lou Stern wheezed.

"Maybe," I said. "It's a kind of a deal I'm offering, but it's a little complicated."

"We'll stay with it!" Sonny rasped.

"I figure Janice's killer has to be one of three people," I explained. "Either it's one of you—or Chris Edwards. Now, I want whoever it was, real bad! So if the four of us get together, my guess is we'll find the killer in no time at all. So the four of us get together over at my house around four this afternoon, right?"

"Oh, sure!" Sonny sneered. "We got nothing better to do than play nutty games over at your house!"

"That's the first half of the deal," I went on blandly, like he'd never spoken. "The second half is, that in return for the innocent parties' cooperation in helping me find the killer, I'm prepared to make them my full partners in unloading that hot ice, on a fifty-fifty basis right down the line!"

"Did you say fifty-fifty?" The strained look on Stern's face was almost pathetic. "Is that what he said, Sonny?" He turned toward West, wheezing for help.

"That's what he said." Sonny nodded, his eyes still not sure he could believe it, even now.

"Mike, old buddy!" For a moment Lou gave a startling imitation of a benevolent buzzard. "We're deeply grateful!"

"Never mind that," I snapped, "just be sure you get over to my house at four this afternoon."

"Don't worry about us, we'll be there." Sonny's eyes glittered again. "You make sure Chris Edwards gets there, and your worries are over, Kluger!"

I got back to the car a couple of minutes later, and slid onto the front seat beside Maggie Smith.

"Did everything go all right in there?" she asked in a breathless voice.

"Just fine," I told her. "The Blue Goose is our next stop."

Her driving was strictly inspired, and it seemed no time at all before she pulled up in front of the club. Then she looked at me for a long moment, and sighed.

"I guess I have to sit here and wait again?"

"It won't take but a minute," I told her. "Just close your eyes and think what your boss will say when he hears how you turned in those diamonds!"

I got out of the car and walked parallel to it until I was level with the rear fender, then dropped down on one knee and pretended to tie a shoelace. The little black box with its pint-sized aerial was about where I figured it would be, neatly clamped to the underside of the car maybe twelve inches back from the fender.

Maggie Smith jumped convulsively when I leaned my head inside the driving window and cleared my throat apologetically.

"You startled me, Mike!" she said. "I thought you were inside the club already."

"When did you last have your car serviced?" I asked her.

"I'm not sure." She stared at me blankly. "Why?"

"There's a little black box stuck on the underside at the back," I explained. "You think it's a bomb, or something?"

The various emotions that collided all over her face made for a fascinating, if brief, diversion.

"Black box?" she said in a strangled voice. "Maybe it's part of the motor, or something?"

"The motor fits under the hood," I said, using the kind of voice you need when you're explaining something to a three-year-old child. "Motors are mechanical devices. The little black box to our rear is from the exciting world of electronics, I believe."

"I hate you, Mike Kluger!" she said savagely.

"I'll say one thing for the Halloran-Smith partnership," I told her. "They never give up!"

"Have you been kidding me along the whole time?" she asked in a choked voice.

"I was a little leary from the start," I admitted, "and I figured that quaint little toy would clinch it. You'd need it in case I'd cached those diamonds under a rock out in the desert someplace, so Halloran could tag along behind, right?"

"If you were so goddamned smart from the beginning," she blurted, "why go along with it all this time?"

"Miss Smith," I said gratefully, "I would like to thank your company through you, their representative, for providing me with a car and chauffeur! This generous—"

There was no point in saying any more. Maggie

had the window shut tight and the motor running by then.

"Sure, Mike!" Chris Edwards said, nodding vigorously. "I'll be over at your house at four this afternoon, you can make book on it!"

"Fine," I told him.

His cold gray eyes had a stab at reading the back of my mind for a few seconds, then gave up reluctantly.

"I know how you feel about Janice O'Brien, baby!" He boomed it at me as an intimate confidence that ricochetted around the walls of the club. "She was a great kid! Great singer, too! We'll miss her, boy! Let me tell you, we'll miss her always."

"You told me," I snarled.

"Watch that punk Sonny West out at your house this afternoon, Mike baby," he bellowed suddenly. "I'll cut him down for you when the time's right, but he's kind of sneaky."

"Sure," I said. "We'll all have a ball watching each other this afternoon, Chris, so make sure you don't miss it, huh?"

I started back toward the door, then that damned moose call hit my ears again.

"Hey, Mike?"

I swung around on my heel and glared death and destruction at him. "What?"

"I know how you feel right now, baby." His voice trembled with emotion, and it sounded like they'd just cut a new subway right under our feet. "All cut and bleeding inside!"

"You told me, already," I groaned.

"But I got to ask you this, boy! You want to take care of her things yourself, or you want me to do it for you, baby?"

"Janice's things?" I stared at him. "The maniac who killed her took care of her things—hacked them into pieces and scattered them all over the apartment!"

"The things in her dressing room, Mike, old buddy!"

A soulful look showed on his face, and his fleshy nose quivered gently. "There's not much down there to remember her by, but what there is belongs to you—if you want it?"

"I'll go take a look," I said, "and—thanks, Chris."

"It's such a little thing to do for you in your hour of grief, boy!" He shook his head mournfully. "You want me to show you the way?"

"Just tell me how to get there," I said, then swallowed bravely. "It's just that—well—at a time like this, I'd rather be alone with her memory, you understand, Chris?"

"I sure do!" He whipped a giant handkerchief out of his pocket and blew his nose emotionally. "She was too young to die, boy! Too young!"

The dressing room was tucked away at the far end of a narrow corridor, and was really just a small cubicle once you got inside. A tarnished mirror was fixed to one wall, and a small dresser stood underneath it. The top was littered with empty lipstick tubes, a large box of cheap powder, a pair of nail scissors, and a comb with half a dozen teeth missing. I opened the drawer and saw it contained a box of tissues and one bronze earring.

A couple of cheap dresses hung listlessly in the closet, and just looking at them could turn me into a manic-depressive, I figured. Then I saw the row of little people sitting crowded together on the top shelf, and brightened up again. There were Kewpie dolls, some cute and some wise, a couple of teddy bears, a teen-age chick with a knowing look and a ponytail. . . . *And you spent around twenty dollars shooting at those bouncing balls on water jets—just to win me a prize to add to my collection!*

I could almost hear the pathetic happiness in Janice O'Brien's voice as she recounted an incident from the happiest day of her whole life.

What was it Diane said? Mike Kluger was very big in amusement parks? So he came back for those vital twenty-four hours, to spend every minute of them with a kid named Janice O'Brien and get his extra kicks from a shooting gallery? That damned paradox was leering at me again. He came to stash away his loot in a safe place, everybody said. Then he spent the whole time with the girl, but he never gave her anything. I looked up at the little people who sat patiently on the shelf again, and held my breath.

Kewpie dolls were made from clay or cheap china, I remembered, and that made them brittle. I took down the two teddy bears and the teen-ager, then reached for the nail scissors on the dresser top. It was brutal surgery and it didn't help, when the sawdust spilled out of the teddy bears' insides, that they still smiled at me with absolute faith in my goodwill.

I didn't feel so bad when it came the teen-age chick's turn. She was kind of asking for it with that knowing look on her face, and the ponytail and all. I jabbed the scissor points into her rounded stomach without a moment's hesitation, then ripped her open all the way up to her china neck. For a moment there, I figured she looked even more knowing, as the precious stones fell onto the dresser top in a glittering cascade.

"That's a real pretty sight, baby!"

I spun around as the booming voice re-echoed around the tiny room, and saw the massive bulk of Chris Edwards filling the doorway.

"Now we're partners, you just leave them right where they are and I'll take good care of them, old buddy!" he roared happily.

"Now, wait a minute!" I said. "You don't—"

He raised his right hand carelessly, and I suddenly found myself looking down the barrel of a thirty-eight.

"No point in arguing, boy!" he thundered. "You can only get hurt that way!"

"Chris," I said slowly. "You didn't kill her, did you?"

"She worked for me, baby." He dropped his voice umpteen decibels in volume, and my ears were grateful. "I could have worked her over at any time. But I liked the kid, and besides, why worry about a broad, when you know—" His eyes widened suddenly as he stared at me vacantly.

"Know what?" I growled.

"Know—" He made a gurgling sound deep in his throat, and his gun-arm dropped down to his side, like it was suddenly tired.

Then he slowly sank onto his knees in a supplicating attitude that lasted maybe a couple of seconds before he fell face down on the floor. I gaped at the haft of a knife protruding from between his shoulder blades, then looked up quickly and saw the cold fury burning in Walter Arndt's soiled brown eyes. He looked at me without speaking for a long moment, then suddenly turned his head and spoke to someone outside in the narrow corridor.

"It's okay," he said thinly. "Come on in."

"I heard the quick footsteps, then a man I'd never seen before in my whole life stepped into the room. He was tall, around my height and weight, I guessed, and about the same age. His thick dark hair was prematurely graying. His face seemed vaguely familiar, and the more I studied it, the more familiar it got, with the same feeling of intimate association you build with a bathroom mirror, I realized suddenly. That was why I felt I knew the guy's face—it looked a lot like the one I shaved every day.

"It must be your turn now to be Mike Kluger?" I said slowly.

"I wouldn't deprive you of that pleasure." He grinned coldly. "My name's Farrel—Mike Farrel!" He glanced briefly at the diamonds piled on top of the dresser. "And I just got rich!"

"You're a lucky man, Mr. Farrel," I told him.

He threw back his head and laughed, and the harsh grating sound filled the room. Then he stopped suddenly.

"You know something, Mr. Kluger?" he sneered softly. "With the kind of problems you got right now, I wouldn't want to change places with you for a min-

ute, even! Not if somebody offered me twenty grand—
and my markers back!"

Walter Arndt knelt down beside Chris Edwards
body, jerked the knife free from his back, then carefully wiped the blade on the dead man's coat.

"I don't mind the cute dialogue, Mike," he said,
with a note of irritation in his voice, "but this is the
wrong place for it!"

"You're right," the real Mike Kluger nodded. "Let's
go back to my house—" He looked up at me and
grinned. "Sorry! I mean—our house!"

chapter nine

My watch said it was two-thirty when we stopped in the driveway, so it looked like I'd missed out on lunch, but then I figured it had been a busy morning, at that. I grinned sourly when I remembered my departing words to Diane, something about how I was going out to raise hell until something happens. The way things were now, it wasn't the return of a prodigal, but more like an avalanche.

Walter Arndt had insisted I drive the car back from the Blue Goose, while he sat behind me in the back seat with a gun in his hand. The real Mike Kluger was beside him, carefully nursing his loot wrapped in one of the cheap dresses from the closet that had belonged to Janice O'Brien.

"You go first, Farrel," Arndt said, once I'd switched off the motor. "Straight into the house, huh? I'll be right in back of you."

"Anything you say, Walter," I told him politely.

"Don't push it!" he said. "Nobody needs you anymore, Farrel. You want to remember that."

I opened the car door and got out, keeping behind it for a couple of seconds, while their attention was fixed momentarily on getting out of the back seat. I had long enough to lift Diane's gun out of my hip pocket and stuff it into the waistband of my pants before I walked into the house.

The fact that Walter Arndt hadn't even bothered to search me to see if I was carrying a gun, had worried me for most of the drive back from Edwards'

club. Then I finally realized the answer was so obvious
I hadn't seen it. The way I'd blown my cash playing
roulette like a gaga honeymooner in Monaco—and on
a rigged wheel at that, where I wouldn't have had a
prayer of coming out ahead—then let myself be talked
into impersonating Kluger, which was the *real* fix—
any of it would have convinced Walter that I was a
sucker, and worse; a spineless punk who didn't have
the guts to fight back. He didn't look to see if I was
carrying a gun, because he was so goddamned sure
the very thought of it, even, would have scared me to
death. I just hoped nothing happened right now to
make him change his mind.

I led a small procession through the front hall into
the living room. Diane was sitting in her usual chair,
her head turned toward the sound of our footsteps.
She had a strained look of concentration on her face.
I guessed she was listening hard, trying to separate
the individual footsteps so she could identify the own-
ers.

"Why, Mr. Farrel," a cool, mocking voice said
lightly, "I'm hurt! Don't you even say hello to your
old friends anymore?"

I looked across at the blonde with the heart-shaped
face, who was leaning casually against the bar with a
drink in one hand. The tall, elegant blonde whose self-
control seemed impregnable, but wasn't always, I suddenly remembered. She wore a stunning white silk-
knit suit with a blouson top, which put her at the top
of the fashion class, even if it did conceal her exciting
sharp-thrusting breasts and molded hips, which I now
remembered with vivid clarity.

"Please say something, Mr. Farrel!" Her sensual
mouth twisted in a sardonic grin. "You look like
you've just seen a ghost or something. Was it that
bad a shock, meeting the real Mike Kluger?"

I smiled politely at her, then turned my head toward the other blonde sitting in the armchair.

"Hey, Diane," I said. "I see your sister Deirdre's
back in town?"

"With my husband," Diane said in a dry voice. "But then life is always full of surprises, I always say!" The corners of her mouth twitched for a moment. "Is that what you always say, Mr. Farrel?"

"Always!" I agreed.

"Just how in hell did you figure out who I was?" Arline Gray said angrily.

"Forget it!" Kluger said. "It's all history now, baby! Feast your eyes on this!"

He dropped the bundled dress onto the coffee table, then opened it with a sudden jerk, so the pile of stones seemed to explode with glittering light.

"Ah!" Arline Gray said from someplace deep in her throat, and the sound expressed something close to sexual gratification.

"A hundred grand, maybe a little more," Kluger said in an exultant voice, "and no problems to go with it—thanks to my good friend, Farrel, hey?"

"You've got more problems than you ever dreamed of, right now, Kluger," I told him.

He didn't even hear me; he was completely absorbed by the pile of uncut diamonds. I looked at Walter Arndt and saw him watching Kluger's blissful face as he stared hypnotically at the jewels. Naked contempt showed momentarily in his dirty brown eyes.

"Kluger I became, and now I stay Kluger forever?" I said. "Is that the idea?"

Arline Gray laughed softly. "It always was, my friend!"

"I was a little stupid not realizing that from the first night I stayed in the penthouse," I said. "You remember how you came naked into my bed moaning something about 'Mike! It's been so long,' and—"

"Shut up!" Arline screamed. "Stop him, Walter?"

"You cut him off right in the middle of the best bit," Arndt sneered. "I don't want to stop him, I want to hear the rest of it!"

"You stinking, lousy—" She darted suddenly from the bar toward Kluger and grabbed his arm. "Shut

him up, Mike! Please, I can't stand it—coming from
that spineless creep!"

"Take it easy, baby," he said, without shifting his
gaze from the diamonds. "Who cares what the punk
says?"

"That's right," Walter said softly, "so knock it off,
will you, Arline? Give the spineless creep a chance to
finish it."

She walked back to the bar unsteadily. She leaned
against it with her back toward me and her shoulders
hunched, as if she expected my words to hit her with
a physical impact.

"None of those incoherent phrases she babbled
meant a thing to me then," I continued. "When she
said, 'All those years it was building up inside me and
I never knew until now,' I figured she'd flipped. But
the way she's built, who'd argue?"

Arline smashed her fist down onto the bar top in
frustrated fury and humiliation. "I'll kill him!" she
moaned. "I swear, Mike Kluger, I'll kill him if you
won't!"

"It was a psycho thing, of course," I said. "I was
about to impersonate the real Mike Kluger—I even
looked a lot like him—and I was available. But maybe
the most interesting bit was that once she started
making love, she suddenly reverted to a seventeen-
year-old kid."

I noted Kluger had overcome the diamond's dead-
ly fascination and was listening hard.

"Yeah?" Walter said encouragingly.

"Her voice—the baby talk—she was almost back
in high school! I didn't know what the hell went on at
the time, but I've got a fair idea now," I said.

"I think we've had enough!" Kluger said. "Shut up
for a while, Farrel, we're sick of hearing your crummy
voice!"

"Maybe we could just change the subject?" I suggested. "I've got this anxious feeling in my stomach
about the future, Mr. Kluger. You couldn't look into
a crystal ball for me, maybe?"

He smiled slowly, and it was wholly malicious. "It's just possible I can make a couple of educated guesses. Mike Farrel is due to disappear into thin air sometime tonight, taking the stones with him, of course."

"But that's not me, is it?" I said.

"No, I'm afraid you're the Kluger that stays right here," he said happily. "The man with so many unanswerable problems, that he suddenly decides the only answer is to quit them completely."

"By putting a bullet into his head?" I asked.

Arline Gray spun round suddenly and looked at me with an exultant expression on her tear-ravaged face. "That's right, creep!" she gloated. "You're due to commit suicide in another five or six hours!"

"After first shooting his wife?" Diane said quietly.

"Don't be ridiculous!" Kluger snapped.

Arline stared at him for a moment, an angry red staining her cheeks. "What's the matter? You scared of telling her the truth, or something?"

"Shut up!" he rasped.

"You're absolutely right, sister, dear," Arline said in a vicious parody of every maiden aunt who ever lived. "It's just that your ever-loving husband doesn't have the guts to say it out loud!"

Kluger moved swiftly, so that I heard the sound of the slap almost before I saw him deliver it. Arline staggered backwards until her spine thumped against the bar, then leaned down on the bar top with her head cradled in her arms and cried—the way a seventeen-year-old girl would cry.

"You had to move up your timetable, Mr. Kluger?" I said casually. "I guess that's why you have to stick around this house until tonight?"

He glared at me for a moment, then a look of genuine interest overcame his irritation. "Just how did you figure that out?"

"While Janice O'Brien was alive, you knew she'd keep her doll collection in her dressing room always, wherever she was. But once she was dead you had to go grab your loot before somebody gave the dolls away, or even got curious about what just might be hidden in one of them."

"Yeah," he said. "But now we got the stones, it doesn't make any real difference."

"I could make a couple of educated guesses about your future," I murmured. "The fact that somebody tortured Janice, and killed her in the process, will make all the difference to you, here and now, and in the immediate future, for example?"

"Now I'm getting tired of listening to him run off at the mouth," Walter Arndt said. "Shut up, Farrel! Go sit down someplace and keep quiet!"

"Now, wait a minute," Kluger said. "He's got me going just here. I want the rest of it."

Walter opened his mouth to say something, then suddenly changed his mind and shrugged his shoulders instead.

"Let's hear the rest, Farrel," Kluger said curtly.

"Who killed Janice O'Brien?" I asked him.

"How the hell do I know!" He lit a cigarette impatiently. "Sonny West most likely—Lou Stern—the two of them together? It could have been Chris Edwards, even!"

"I walked into the apartment with her," I said, "and got slugged over the back of the head. While I was out on the floor, the killer started working over Janice. Why?"

"He figured she had my diamonds—or she knew where they were—what else!"

"But Stern, West, and Edwards, all believed I was you—Mike Kluger!" I said. "And if one person in the whole world knew for sure where Mike Kluger had hidden his loot, it would be Kluger himself, right?"

"So why didn't they work you over?" He nodded slowly. "Hey! You're right—that lets them out?"

"Whoever it was, only picked on the girl because they *knew* I was a fake!" I emphasized each word. "How many people knew that, Mr. Kluger?"

"Arline," he whispered, "me—" He turned toward Arndt, his face darkening. "And you—Walter?"

"And me!" Walter smiled faintly, and the gun in his hand traversed a gentle arc that included both me and Kluger.

"Why?" Kluger asked in an incredulous voice.

"I picked up Arline three years back, in a Greenwich Village bar," Arndt said. "She looked like something from outer space, but she had a lot of style. The guy that owned the bar had her working as a shill among the bohemian types, and it was costing him money because they didn't drink that much anyway. But he was grooming her for bigger things, ready for when he went into the junk-peddling business.

"I took her out of that. I spent a lot of time and money to make her what she is—or was, up until a couple of months back! She had a whole bunch of talent, and when it was groomed right, it blossomed like a rose. She's a full partner in my gambling operation back home, did you know that, Kluger? You got any idea how much that partnership is worth to her in five years from now?"

Walter sneered at him. "No—you wouldn't! A penny-ante heist man who figures seven years in San Quentin in exchange for a bag of hot ice—if he can keep his hands on it!—is a big deal? When she first told me she'd been writing you in the pen, and the background to it, I figured it was worth a try. I didn't mind taking the hot ice, not when somebody else had done the time for it! But the first time she visited you in San Quentin, she went clean out of her mind! The way Farrel just told it—acting like a kid again, crazy for you, like you was something, even!

"So I still went along with it because there was no choice. I even went along with this maniac idea you both had of providing a fake Kluger to give all the bloodhounds a bum steer—so when it was right, you could sneak in, grab your hot ice, and sneak out again without anybody ever knowing. And Farrel—the patsy—would be left here to try and prove he wasn't you.

"Then Arline told me we were washed up, and once

you had the loot, the two of you would take off permanently. I wasn't about to let that happen! I said I'd run observation right here for you—bring you up to date on what was happening in the town seven years later—and that way I found out the O'Brien dame was back in town to meet you when you got out.

"It figured it had to be her you'd given the ice to, for safekeeping until you got back, so I figured on beating you to the jump! A couple of things went against me; you'd been cute enough to give the dame the ice without her knowing she had it, even, and nobody told me she had a bum heart!"

The only sound in the room when Arndt finished speaking was the ragged sound of Arline's harsh breathing, as she dragged herself up from the bar top and walked toward him. Her intention was made crystal-clear by the murderous fury which twisted her face into a savage mask of destruction.

"Kluger's no good for you, baby," Walter said. "A punk like him just isn't worth dying for—it would be a waste!"

"I'm going to kill you, Walter," she said in a blurred voice. "You can't stop me!"

"A thirty-eight slug at this range won't only stop you, honey," he said with brutal logic, "it'll even stop your cousin Louis from Eagle Falls, Montana, right in back of you, too!"

"Walter's right, Arline!" I said quickly. "Any way it comes out, you lose. You're seven years too old for Mike Kluger, already!

chapter ten

Arline stopped dead in her tracks, thrown off balance by the fast curve I'd just thrown her, and I nearly sobbed with relief. If she had kept on going, I would have had no choice but to make a grab for the gun tucked into the waistband under my buttoned jacket. The chances of getting it clear before Walter Arndt put a bullet between my eyes, were a million-to-one against, I figured.

Still painfully vivid in my memory was how Chris Edwards had stood facing me for at least ten seconds after Walter plunged the knife into his back. It was a long time for a man to be dying on his feet, and I hadn't realized it was happening until his knees buckled under him. I kept wondering if Chris had known, either.

"Too old?" Arline snarled. "What do you mean, too *old!*"

"Kluger was the first guy you ever had?" I asked, and she nodded vaguely. "It happened when you were seventeen and just a teen-age chick. When you ran away to New York, he figured maybe it didn't have to be a total loss, because you had an older sister. And she was still a teen-age chick!"

"He was the first man I ever had, too!" Diane whispered.

"After seven years, Janice O'Brien hadn't forgotten the one night she spent with Mike Kluger," I rasped. "She couldn't have been any more than eighteen at the time, either. Add another to the list of

teen-age chicks! 'You made me a woman that night,'
were the exact words she used, as I remember?"

"Stop it!" Arline moaned. "I won't listen!"

"Walter," I snapped. "You saw the doll—the one
he'd hidden the diamonds in?"

"Sure, I did," he acknowledged.

"Tell Arline what it looked like?"

"It was a doll!" He moved his shoulders in sup-
pressed irritation. "I don't know, it was kind of cute
maybe—a ponytail and all—come-hither eyes that
looked a little too old for it and—of course!—a teen-
age doll, what else?"

"I—won't—listen!" Arline swung her head violently between each word.

"You should listen good," I snarled at her, "if you
don't want to wind up in a nuthouse! It's a simple
enough pattern. For Kluger they've got to be young,
and he's got to be the first. After that, he loses interest. Once he's got his hundred grand out of those
diamonds, how long do you think you'd last against
the competition of all the seventeen-year-old chicks
who'll see him as the big-deal older man, handsome
and sophisticated, and the biggest spender they ever
met in their whole lives before!"

Arline's face tightened into a mask of single-minded
purpose again and I tensed, watching Walter Arndt
out of the corner of my eye, but she headed straight
toward Kluger instead.

"Filth!" she mumbled, and a string of obscenities
followed. "First me—and then my sister—and that
poor kid, Janice O'Brien—and how many more now
you're free again?"

"Lay off, Arline!" Kluger said hoarsely. "I've taken
about all I'm going to take, right now." The sweat
ran streaming down his face, and his body shivered
spasmodically about every ten seconds.

"You're wrong, Kluger!" I laughed at him, with the
same kind of repellent sound in my voice that had
been in his when he'd laughed at me in Janice's dressing room. "There's a mountain of dirt waiting to be

eaten yet!" I told him. "Like Walter said, you set me up as the patsy and he went along with it. But everything's changed now. We got a new patsy, Kluger. This is a live one! Pulled a heist and stashed away the loot, then did seven years—get that?—seven *years* in the pen. Then, inside the first three days he's out, he loses the dame who was minding the loot for him, the dame who was helping him get hold of it, and the loot itself!"

"The biggest patsy of all time!" Even Walter Arndt allowed himself the luxury of a chuckle. "You'll go down in history: Kluger, the all-time patsy!"

As Arndt finished speaking, Arline got within striking distance and lashed out suddenly, dragging her nails viciously down the side of his face, so they left furrows of blood and torn skin in their wake.

It was Kluger's breaking point. He screamed wildly from the depths of his fear, hatred, greed, and guilt; then suddenly he saw something tangible to revenge himself upon within reach. He grabbed Arline by the throat and started to throttle her.

"Let go of her, Kluger!" Walter yelled at him. "Or I'll let you have it!"

The menace in his voice was strong enough to penetrate even Kluger's wild fury; it forced him to lift his head quickly. For a couple of seconds he stared blankly at Arndt; then the veins knotted in his forehead as he made a supreme effort of strength, and literally threw Arline at him.

It was the unexpectedness of the move that tossed Walter, I figured afterwards. A body suddenly whirling through the air toward him—and his finger tensed on the trigger. His gun exploded, firing two shots so fast that there was only one blur of sound.

The impact as the two slugs hit made Arline's body hesitate in mid-air for a fraction of a second, before it slammed into Walter's chest, driving him to the floor. The gun spun wildly out of his hand, hit the floor, and skidded toward Kluger. I grabbed frantically for the gun tucked inside my waistband, fumbled with the butt until I got a decent grip, then yanked hard and fouled the barrel in the waistband again. A spectator would have figured it was hilarious, but for me it was stark tragedy, as I watched Kluger dive onto Walter's gun, then scramble back onto his feet again with the butt held firmly in his right hand.

"Patsy, hey, Farrel?" He chuckled gleefully. "We'll see who's the patsy! The guy full of holes, that's who!"

I gave a last, despairing tug and heard a sudden tearing sound, then the gun was clear. We fired simultaneously, and I saw the flash from Kluger's gun so vividly, I figured I must have been looking straight down the barrel, and any moment now my head would be brutally detached from my shoulders. Only it didn't happen.

For one dreadful moment as I watched Kluger fall to the floor, with blood pouring from the gaping hole just beneath his left eye, I had a feeling of utter conviction that destiny had decreed it was not Mike Kluger who should die, but Mike Farrel. That was why it had decreed I should first become Mike Kluger by impersonation. I waited helplessly for the moment when I would find myself trapped inside the dying body of Kluger, with no escape, and somewhere inside my mind I could hear myself screaming.

Then Kluger's body hit the floor, rolled over to one side, and went limp. The reaction, and the release from that living nightmare, almost buckled my knees under me. I felt my whole body tremble while I kept saying to myself that it was all over—finished!

I was still saying it when Walter Arndt's thin voice sounded in my ears like the crack of doom.

"Drop the gun, Farrel," he said, "or I'll run it through her neck like a skewer!"

My head turned sideways, an inch at a time, with the jerky movement of a mechanical doll. Then I saw him standing behind Diane's chair, the point of the knife he'd used to kill Chris Edwards held tight against the side of her neck. My fingers straightened in an automatic reflex, and the gun hit the floor.

"Now kick it over here," he said.

I did as he said, and the gun stopped a foot away from him, so it was within easy reach when he stooped down and picked it up.

"If I'd been smart I would have given it to you right after I gave it to Edwards," he said. "I had you all wrong, Farrel, figured you for a punk! You must have been carrying that gun the whole time, and I didn't even frisk you."

He laughed mirthlessly. "You want to know the real patsy in all this? It's me! And you made it come out that way. Working on Arline first, so you'd get my support against her and Kluger. Then working on me, so Kluger would be on your side—and I let you get away with it?" He shook his head in disbelief. "So what's left for me? Nothing!" His voice shook momentarily. "Arline's dead—and because of your lousy conniving and double talk, it worked out so it was me who killed her. The gambling house and everything else gone. Nobody could beat this rap!" He stared vacantly at the two bodies on the floor for a brief second. "Then there's the O'Brien broad, and Edwards."

His dark brown eyes were the dirtiest thing in the whole world when he looked at me right then. "Nothing left but revenge, Farrel," he whispered. "You figure I'm going to shoot you now?"

"Right," I said, because it was a stupid question.

"Wrong!" He smiled. "This broad—Diane, huh?—I watched the two of you. Something going on there, Farrel, I could feel it, and it wasn't the usual big-deal sympathy bit just because she's blind, either. So I've got great news for you, Farrel! I'm going to let you stand there and watch, while the knife goes into her neck, an inch at a time!"

There was an expectant glint in his repulsive eyes which faded slowly as he realized I wasn't about to have a violent reaction for his amusement.

"You don't have to just stand there, Farrel, when she starts screaming," he said generously. "You could try jumping me instead! I'd like that, because then I can put a slug—"

Walter was calling the shots so I figured he'd be right about most anything, but the hell with allowing him the luxury of guessing right about something where I had free choice. So I jumped him right then—while he was still talking.

It was stupid from the start because the distance between us was too great, over ten feet, but it was preferable to just standing there watching him murder Diane, knowing my own turn came next.

The moment after I'd made the convulsive leap, it was like someone had pulled a master switch, and the next moment the whole world moved in slow motion. It gave me all the time I needed, and more, to watch Walter's every movement as I sailed gently toward him, with no more velocity than a coal barge in a fitful breeze.

I saw his first incredibly fast reaction, controlled purely by reflexes; the sudden glint in his eyes as intelligence took over, calculating relative speed, and my vulnerability. Then finally debating the target area—the decision canting the gun barrel a fraction, while my stomach lurched with fear.

Suddenly, everything speeded up and returned to normal, and I was hurtling through the air toward him, but it was still too slow to do any good. About three feet away, I watched his finger tighten on the trigger, then the sound of the shot hammered against my eardrums. I made a wild guess that I was already too close to see the flash, then a second shot hammered my eardrums again.

The gun barrel wavered for a split second, then slewed sideways a couple of inches as the third shot exploded in the room. For the first time I saw the flash, then my shoulder slammed into his chest and we crashed onto the floor. Arndt was underneath me as we hit, and I had both hands locked around his throat, intent on strangling him to death in the shortest time possible.

A couple of seconds after we landed, I reluctantly had to admit to myself that his body was limp already, and most likely had been that way before we reached the floor. My hands relaxed their grip on his throat, and I rolled sideways to get clear, then came up onto my knees. There were two neat holes in the side of his head, so close together they almost touched.

I got up onto my feet without hurrying, mainly because sailing in slow motion toward a gun barrel pointing straight at you just isn't the kind of sport to relax your nerve ends, not on a temporary basis, anyway! Lieutenant Cromby stood in the doorway, his gun still in his hand, and gave me a vague nod when I looked in his direction.

"Lieutenant?" Diane cried out suddenly, as if she was in pain.

"Sure, I'm here, honey," Cromby said in a warm, reassuring voice. "I'm fine!"

"Thank God!" Diane slumped back in her chair with a wonderful look of mingled happiness and gratitude on her face. Then maybe ten whole seconds later she said, "Mike Farrel?" and it sounded like an afterthought.

"I'm just fine," I told her.

"That's nice," she murmured approvingly. "I would have felt so badly if you'd been killed, after we set you up the way we did!"

"We?" I yelped.

"Arthur—I mean, Lieutenant Cromby, and me!" Her plump cheeks dimpled delightfully. "I called him as soon as you left to meet Janice O'Brien, you know? He thought it was a wonderful chance to use you in helping him recover the diamonds and trap the real Mike Kluger!"

"He did, huh?" I glared savagely at Cromby, who seemed completely unmoved.

"The lieutenant said we had to keep you moving the whole time though," Diane added. "Like you have to keep a mule moving, by jabbing a sharp-pointed stick into his sides?"

"Or just for a change, give them a boot in the—" I closed my eyes for a moment. "If I'd had the time, I would have been curious about a couple of things, Lieutenant. Like how you just happened to walk into Hagan's Bar a couple of minutes after Janice left? And, even though she was murdered at three-thirty A.M.— why didn't you get here to question me before ten?"

"We figured you had to have some sleep, Farrel," he said seriously. "There was no need to overdo it, of course."

"That bit on the doorstep!" I groaned in anguish at the memory. "The genius lieutenant wondering why seven years in the pen had done so much for Mike Kluger!"

"I thought that was pretty damned good myself," he said smugly. "Especially the punch line—'Now you look worried'!"

I glared down at Diane's sunny face, and resisted a sudden fierce impulse to twist her nose. "Then you made it a point-counterpoint bit right afterwards," I said bitterly. "Sneering at me in your own genteel way, deliberately making me mad so I'd go out and start something! 'Don't be so juvenile!' " I nodded vigorously. "That was the one that did it."

"Then the whole thing nearly blew straight through the roof," Cromby said. "Diane called me and said you'd gone out hell-raising. So I said: Fine! Let me know if he's had any luck, as soon as possible after he gets back. Five minutes after she'd hung up from that call, Kluger, Deirdre—"

"I would prefer you called her Arline Gray," Diane said steadily.

"—Arline Gray, and Arndt, moved into the house," Cromby continued. "The two men went to pick up the diamonds, and left the girl here to make sure Diane didn't use the phone. Where did they find you, by the way, Farrel?"

"I was the genius who'd just found the diamonds, with Chris Edwards and a gun right in back of me!"

I said. "Then the other two arrived. Arndt knifed Edwards, and they brought me back here."

"It was your hell-raising that paid off," he grunted. "You made Lou Stern and Sonny West some wild proposition? Said it was one of them, or Chris Edwards, who'd killed the O'Brien girl, and you wanted the killer real bad—"

"Hey! That's right!" I said. "They should have been here at four o'clock—sharp!" I looked at my watch, and saw it was after five. "What happened?"

"Those two don't even trust each other," he said, grinning, "so they didn't trust you for a minute. They decided to drop into the Blue Goose for a confidential chat with Edwards before they came over here. When they found his body, they figured you'd killed him for sure, and they couldn't get to a phone fast enough to tell me!"

"I'm glad they didn't sneeze, or anything," I said thankfully. "You cut it so fine, you had me walking a razor's edge already!"

"I saved your life, Farrel!" he said, in mild protest.

"I'm not complaining about that," I admitted. "I'm just complaining about how you took your own goddamn time to do it!"

The phone rang around seven the following evening, and I answered it leisurely.

"Cromby," the lieutenant's voice said crisply. "How's everything at the house, Farrel?"

"Just fine," I said truthfully. "The cleaners took the rugs this morning, so now you wouldn't even know a single drop of blood had been spilled anywhere."

"Oh, great!" he said dryly. "I appreciate you looking after the house while Diane is away. With that final operation due in ten days, I think it's important she should get a change of scenery, and a rest. Especially after everything that's just happened!"

"You talk like her husband already!" I told him.

His laugh sounded faintly embarrassed: "I do have a small personal problem here, at that! In spite of the kind

of man Kluger was, and the hard facts that out of a
marriage that lasted seven years, she only spent the
first six weeks of it with him, I still can't forget he's
only been dead for twenty-four hours. If there weren't
any unusual circumstances I'd happily wait a few
months before I—"

"But right now she's got that final operation coming
up ten days from now," I said, "and you want to ask
her to marry you before that? So she'll never have any
doubts that you want to marry her, whatever the out-
come of the operation?"

"That's exactly the problem!" he said.

"I don't think you have any problem, Lieutenant," I
said. "The sickening way she'd drool every time your
name was mentioned over the last couple of days nearly
sent me out of my mind! You'll be in trouble if you
don't ask soon, is all."

"Well, thanks!" His voice was suddenly a lot brighter.
"I handed over the Kluger diamonds officially to the insurance company's representative, as you requested,
and told them you get the reward."

"That's real nice of you, Lieutenant!"

"Well, I figured as we used you as kind of undercover
agent—even if you didn't know it at the time—you
should get some compensation! You would have appreciated the look on the other investigator's face!"
He chuckled richly. "It was a classic!"

"I can imagine," I told him.

"I guess that's about it," he said. "What will you do
with all that reward money, Farrel? You're not going
to play any more roulette, I hope?"

"Don't worry about that!" I said confidently. "I'm
cured for all time. No more roulette! A little poker,
maybe—"

For some nutty reason of his own, he was laughing
in an hysterical, ridiculous kind of way when I hung
up.

Maybe an hour later a gray sedan pulled into the
drive, and the doorbell rang imperiously. When I
opened the door, a girl with a raven's wing of rich

jet-black hair swooping across her head, wearing a shapeless black raincoat buttoned up to her neck, stared at me solemnly without saying a word.

For a moment I figured the look in her dark eyes was one of undisguised adoration, then common sense said it was a trick of the lousy porch light.

"Hi, Maggie," I said tentatively.

"Mike Farrel, I positively adore you!" she purred. "When the police lieutenant handed me the diamonds and said they were recovered almost solely due to the efforts of Mr. Farrel, who was entitled to the reward, I got so excited I nearly died!"

She sighed blissfully. "But when he gave me that letter addressed to the president of the company himself! The one you wrote, saying you strongly doubted if the diamonds would have been recovered by you, had it not been for the intelligent and resourceful help offered gladly at all times by one of their own investigators, Miss Margaret Smith—" she closed her eyes in sheer ecstasy "—you should have seen the look on Halloran's face!"

"What did he do?"

"Went out and shot himself, I shouldn't be surprised!" she said gleefully. "Who cares? I bet he'll make sure he never works with me again, and amen to that!"

"Won't you come in and have a drink or something?" I said.

Her face was suddenly solemn again. "I'm sorry I forgot to mention it before, Mr. Farrel, but I'm here on official business."

She bent down with one hand waving behind her back, then straightened up again and produced a large, slightly battered suitcase with a flourish.

"I have brought your reward, Mr. Farrel!" she said in a ringing voice.

"Thanks a bunch!" I stared at the suitcase for a couple of seconds, then mentally shrugged. If a company the size of Global thought the correct way to deliver twenty thousand dollars was to send it out in a battered suitcase, who the hell was I to argue with them, especially when I hadn't got my hands on the loot yet?

"I need to make some small preparations for the informal ceremony which always goes with this reward, Mr. Farrel," Maggie said stiffly. "Would you please let me have a few minutes alone in the living room?"

"Sure," I said blankly.

"Thank you!"

She picked up the suitcase and went past me toward the living room, then stopped for a moment in the doorway.

"Oh, Mr. Farrel?"

"Yeah!" I growled.

"Please hold yourself in readiness, so that when you hear your name called, you can proceed straight into the room!"

The door closed firmly, wiping out the sight of the sickly-sweet smile on her face. I wondered if the letter I'd written her company president had inspired her to become one of those real dedicated career girls? I knew one once. She wouldn't sleep with anybody *outside* the company because it would only mean a nonproductive effort. She wouldn't sleep with anybody *inside* the company, below the rank of vice-president, because it would only mean a misguided effort.

"Mr. Farrel?" I heard a voice call faintly from inside the living room. "You may come in now!"

I slammed open the door and marched grimly into the living room, then found myself instantly transported into the middle of a vast desert of darkness. Then, a moment later, I saw the friendly lights of an oasis in the far corner of the room and started toward them.

In no time at all, it seemed, I stood on the edge of the oasis, panting a little, while I gazed at the delights displayed in front of my very eyes. A magic wand had been waved, and an ordinary couch had been transformed, by someone tossing a black velvet drape over it, into a sumptuous throne of love. A leopard-skin rug, placed carefully in front of the couch, added an exotic dash of spice to the scene, while soft music played all around in sensual rhythms.

The masterpiece of the whole creation lay back in wanton repose against rich black velvet, like a priceless pearl displayed in a jewelbox. I studied her carefully and noticed how the soft light played tricks with its shadows. The raven's wing looked tousled, as if it was tumbling down over her head and across one eye. The sharp planes of her face looked enticing, rather than intelligent; her broad mouth, which I had always thought of as strongly humorous, was now purely provocative.

But the light and shade couldn't play tricks with everything, I realized gratefully. The halter top of her white bikini pajamas still couldn't conceal the ripe perfection of her high breasts, and the minute briefs attempted nothing more than to emphasize, with maybe a touch of modest pride, the riotous curves of her hips.

"Well?" the priceless pearl said suddenly, in a challenging tone of voice.

"I think it's magnificent," I told her, while I was busy searching under the leopard-skin rug.

"You're sure? I mean, you really approve?"

"I'm just crazy about the whole deal," I mumbled, then plunged my hand blindly into the ice bucket which held the champagne, and yelped as the wet ice chilled my fingers.

"What are you?" she asked in a suspicious voice. "Some kind of a party-games nut?"

"Okay!" I bared my teeth at her. "You've had your fun. So where is it?"

"Where's what?"

"My reward!" I listened to a dreadful whimpering sound for a couple of seconds, then realized it was me. "Don't kid around with twenty thousand dollars, honey!" I pleaded.

"Oh—that?" She shrugged. "You'll get a check in the mail sometime in the next couple of weeks."

"But you said—"

"You're all confused, Mike!" She gave me that sweet smile routine again. "What I've brought you is the Maggie Smith Personal Reward, and—believe me!—it has absolutely nothing to do with Global Insurance!"

She raised her arms slowly, and the magnificent swell of her breasts rose with them. I watched her fingers interlace at the back of her head, then she lay back against the rich black velvet and made a contented, purring sound.

I tried to hum a little tune myself, but my breathing was ragged enough already, so it didn't actually sound like a tune at all—more like asthma. Then I happened to glance down casually, and found myself looking straight into her dark eyes. They suddenly sparkled, and glowed warmly with the bold promise of unlimited delight.

"You mentioned there was a small, informal ceremony?" I said in a kind of eager hoarseness. "If you don't mind me asking—just when, exactly does it start?"

A low, gurgling laugh came from the husky depths of her throat, and it was the most wicked, abandoned sound I had ever heard in my whole life.

"What do you want, Mike?" Maggie asked in a ribald, mocking voice. "I should blow a bugle, or something?"